Dolly Dearest

The baby doll started smacking its lips in the same way it would when it wanted a bottle, only this time with a feverish intensity Sabrina had never seen it display before. Its mouth pulsed rapidly, like an image on a VHS tape being fast-forwarded. It thrashed its arms and legs, beating them against Sabrina's side. She was alarmed at the impact of its little hands and feet.

And then a searing pain shot through her arm.

The doll had bitten her.

She yelped and flung the baby from her arms. It flipped through the air and then landed with a thud on the driveway, mere feet from the puddle of blood.

Other Terrorcore Rewind paperbacks you will enjoy:

Swing of the Axe
  by G.D. Bowlin

The Hushed Boys
  by Caleb J. Pecue

The Stuffing
  by Austin Hinderliter

The Magician
  by Vanessa Leonardo

A.D. Aro

No part of this publication may be reproduced in whole or in part, or stored in a retrieval system, or transmitted in any form or by any means, electronic, mechanical, photocopying, recording, or otherwise, without written permission of the publisher. For information regarding permission, write to Terrorcore Publishing LLC, 119 Homestead Ct., Edwardsville, Illinois 62025.

ISBN 978-1-970298-90-1

Copyright © 2026 by A.D. Aro. All rights reserved. Published by Terrorcore Publishing LLC. REWIND is a retro-inspired line of nostalgic horror YA books. These books are suitable for kids thirteen or older. For more information regarding content, please email terrorcorepublishing@gmail.com or visit our website at: www.terrorcorepublishing.com/contact.

12 11 10 9 8 7 6 5 4 3 2 1 0

Cover art by Creepy Carves Design.

Printed in the U.S.A.

First Terrorcore printing, April 2026

For Grandma,
Thank you for the typewriter, the belief and all the weekend trips to the mall for new books.

She is remarkable. Her poise, her grace, the way she carries herself. All summer long, I've watched her. Studied her. Learned her routines and habits.

She is like clockwork. I could set my watch to her rhythms. To the way she moves about. How she glides effortlessly, like a beautiful phantom, through the summer haze. Depending on the time of day, I know exactly where she will be.

By 6 AM, she is in front of the mirror, meticulously brushing her long, auburn hair. She takes her looks seriously. She cares about how she presents herself.

If it's the afternoon, anywhere between 2 to 4 PM, you can find her at cheering practice. Despite it being summer vacation, she continues to hone her skills. She is the head cheerleader, and it's easy to see why. Her body is immaculate. School spirit flows through her like the blood in her veins. Her green eyes shimmer with pride as she shakes her pom poms above her head.

Nighttime can be tricky. It depends on what day of the week it is. It took me the entire month of June to learn and memorize all the intricacies of her nocturnal schedule. At 5 PM, she has dinner with her parents, unless it is Friday or Saturday. On Fridays, she likes to go out with her friends.

Sometimes they frolic on down to the beach or hang by the pool, but their favorite haunt is the mall.

I follow as they try on clothes and giggle with gossip. They never notice me. Why would they? Each time I'm wearing a different disguise. To them, I'm nothing more than another shopper.

I like to watch her laugh and be free. To be amongst her peers. She doesn't realize that time is so fleeting. That her youthful joy has an expiration date.

That she has been selected.

Saturdays, she usually reserves for her boyfriend, Christopher. I don't know what she sees in him. Maybe she is dazzled by his sleek red car or his wavy blond hair, but he doesn't fool me. He is so far beneath her. So unworthy of even a glance at her shoes.

At some point, he will need to be taken care of. I can't have him getting in the way. She can't have any distractions. Nothing can hinder the plan.

She is the one. I have ensured that.

She is stunning. I wish I could crawl into her flesh. I wish I could move beneath her bones. To feel what it's like to have her body. Her mind. Her soul. Her name.

Sabrina.

She is the perfect vessel.

Chapter 1

Sabrina Quinn eyed herself in the mirror and held the choker necklace across her throat. It was a thin, black velvet collar with the golden head of a lioness as a charm. The lioness shimmered under the vanity lights that lined the outer edge of her mirror, its mouth open in a permanent roar, its teeth forever on display. With a devilish smirk, she clasped the button at the back, snugging the jewelry tightly around her neck.

Satisfied, Sabrina stood to admire her new look. She'd grown so tired of the perfect preppy image she'd maintained her entire life. Of the rigid structure. Of feeling like she always had to please everyone but herself. By now, getting straight A's was as easy as breathing. She hardly had to think about it. And unless something drastic happened academically, it was already practically set in stone that she would be valedictorian for the Thompson Point High School graduating class of 1995.

In place of her usual turtlenecks and cardigans, Sabrina had opted for a deep cut black V-neck tee accentuated with a light denim jacket. Instead of corduroy pants, she went with a black and white plaid skirt. Her hair was pulled up and away from her face, and her eyes were ringed with dark eyeliner. The choker was the final, but probably most important, piece of the ensemble.

There was a fierceness to the lioness charm that Sabrina hoped to carry with her into senior year. Like the exit of her birth month, she was far too much a lamb. It was time to bring a little bit of lion — or rather lioness — into her life. To roar into senior year with a whole new energy.

Rachel and Christopher are gonna lose it when they see me! Sabrina thought, leaning closer to the mirror to apply some crimson lipstick. She hadn't told either of them about her plans.

Rachel Stockworth had been her best friend since sixth grade and was normally the one Sabrina spilled all her secrets to. As for Christopher Tolter, star quarterback of the football team, they'd only been dating for a few months. He hadn't yet earned the right to be privy to her secrets.

There were other things she hadn't told them. Things that sent an icy chill up Sabrina's spine as she thought of them. Things she was trying to forget or pretend never actually happened.

And that was the tough part. That was the reason she'd never mentioned anything to Rachel or Christopher. Or her parents. Sabrina briefly considered calling the police to file a report, but the problem was she had no *proof*. Who would believe that someone had been stalking her all summer without evidence?

She'd seen a shadowy figure in her bushes more than once. But it was always out of the corner of her eye, a ghostly mist on her periphery. Never any detail, never anything concrete. No footprints left behind. No markings. Nothing.

There were some nights, as Sabrina brushed her hair before bed, when she swore she could hear someone singing a lullaby outside her window. It was always the faintest whisper, barely there, sung so softly it made her question whether it was even truly there. Sabrina did her best to ignore it. She turned on her radio. She blasted her TV. She cranked the A/C. Despite that, etched along the fringe of all the noise, she continued to hear: *"rock-a-bye baby, on the treetop, when the wind blows, the cradle will rock . . ."*

Whoever it was, they were very good at disappearing. Every time Sabrina gathered the courage and either opened her bedroom window to look or pressed her ear to the glass, she saw and heard nothing. Crickets. A nightly summer breeze weaving through the bushes. Raccoons scavenging trash barrels for scraps.

During cheer practice or shopping trips, when she was surrounded by people and her mind was focused on something else, Sabrina felt silly about it all. A stalker singing lullabies in her bushes? Who would do such a thing? And why? Surely she was imagining it.

Though, deep down, she knew she wasn't.

Someone or *something* had been out there. Part of her wondered if it was Lawrence Watkins. Sabrina knew he'd had a crush on her since the eighth grade, and he was always staring at her. She'd hardly spoken more than a few words to him, but something about his quiet demeanor creeped her out. He'd always been a little odd, but that didn't automatically mean he was stalking her, right?

Sabrina shook the thoughts away, giving herself one last inspection in the mirror. She smacked her lips together and winked at her reflection. She hoped that with a new school year beginning, whatever had happened over the summer would fizzle away. That she could forget about the shadows and the lullabies.

Daydreams of all the things she was looking forward to during senior year flooded into her mind, ushering out the memories of her summer stalker. Sabrina smiled as she pictured the big homecoming game, pom poms in hand, leading the cheerleaders while Christopher drove the football team to victory. She could envision cruising to the celebratory party afterward, her hair whipping in the wind from the open window of Christopher's red Nissan 300ZX. She couldn't wait to taste her first beer. To feel the buzz by a bonfire. To relish the win with Christopher's arms around her. The cheerleading queen and the football king.

She pumped the brakes on the imagination train. For a moment, her daydream had shifted to Christopher's hot lips on her neck, his left hand under her skirt, his fingers spider-walking up her thigh, the heat between them as unbearable as a sweltering July sun.

Sabrina sucked in a mouthful of air, trying to steady her fast-beating heart. She was ready for some changes, but going all the way? That was a line she wasn't entirely sure she wanted to cross just yet. Maybe once the lioness had taken hold, but that was a big maybe.

"One change will lead to another," Sabrina told herself. She took a last look around her bedroom, then grabbed her backpack and headed for the living room.

Alteration was the actual word Sabrina kept using in her head. This new look, this new attitude, it wasn't so much a change as it was an *alteration*. She was still Sabrina. Straight A, pom pom pumping, valedictorian Sabrina. She didn't think it was possible to change all of that. But things were going to be on her terms.

The new Sabrina, this alteration, felt less like a secret and more like a statement. It wasn't something she felt should be announced. She didn't want Rachel or Christopher's opinions to hamper her execution, or worse, become her own. No, this was something that they had to see without any prior knowledge. Sabrina wanted to surprise *everyone*.

Chapter 2

Her parents had already left for work by the time she made it downstairs. As Sabrina passed through the kitchen, she noticed a note from her mom on the table, wishing her the best day ever. Scribbled across the bottom, right below the words "Love, Mom", was one of her little catchphrases: *Success is in how you dress!*

Sabrina tossed the note aside and pretended to gag. If there was one thing she'd be glad to be rid of once college came along, it was her parents' constant mantras. Her mom's especially. She constantly regurgitated these mottos as if they were the hidden key to living a perfect life.

High grades never fade!
Honesty always, and you'll never have to lie!
A smile on your face can take you any place!

And her dad's favorite: *Clean face, clean house, clean spirit.*

When she was younger, Sabrina held onto these sayings wholeheartedly. She followed them, obeyed them as if they were non-negotiable rules permanently etched in stone. They had no doubt shaped her into the person she was now. But after seventeen years, it had become nauseating. Coming across more like a constant nagging than a nudge in the right direction. She knew it stemmed from a place of love, but how much could a teenage girl take?

Before stepping out the front door, she caught her reflection in the mudroom mirror. She smiled, running her fingers across the lioness charm as it glistened in the morning light seeping through the window.

New face, new . . .

No, that wouldn't work. She didn't have a new house. Sabrina burst into laughter. A minute later, she composed herself and took a deep, relaxing breath. She stole a final glance in the mirror and, satisfied with what she saw, waved to her reflection and set off.

"New face, new *outfit*, new spirit!" she said aloud before opening the door.

Sabrina strolled across the front lawn, opened the driver's side door of her silver 1989 Ford Taurus, and whipped her backpack onto the passenger seat before climbing in. She started the car and eased it down the driveway, swiveling her head to ensure there were no other cars coming before backing into the street. It wasn't until a few minutes later, as the familiar shapes of the neighborhood houses and trees whisked by on the edge of her periphery and the welcome sign for Thompson Point High School loomed in the distance, that it truly hit her.

Her senior year.

The finality of it all struck like a boulder through the windshield. An invisible fist seemed to punch Sabrina in the stomach. She sucked in a breath and held it, momentarily unaware the car was slowing to a crawl from the release of her foot off the gas pedal. The car behind her beeped angrily. She caught herself, waving apologetically into the rearview mirror as she pressed her foot down and brought the car back up to the allowed speed limit of 35MPH.

The two-story brick building came into view, rising out of a low hill. She could see a string of cars and buses cruising up the winding road that led to the school.

This is it.

There was now a finite number of times she was going to take this morning commute. There was a set number of days in which she could bask in the recognizable ritual of her high school life. The faraway childhood ruminations of the future were over. The future was *now*. It was here.

Sabrina couldn't help but suddenly feel like she was dangling from the edge of a cliff. Teetering on the precipice of youth, the oncoming rush of adulthood biting at her like a feral wind. She struggled to hang on, her fingernails digging into jagged rocks. Her strength wouldn't last forever.

Before she knew it, she'd be walking across that stage to accept her diploma. She'd give her valedictorian speech to a round of applause, and then, after her last true teenage summer break, she'd be off to college. She'd already accepted an offer from the University of Pennsylvania, where she was going for a business degree.

And it wasn't that Sabrina wasn't excited about the next chapter; she was. In that moment, everything seemed so sudden, so immediate. Things were happening now, life was truly in motion, like a ball tumbling down a long flight of stairs. The thoughts came in fast stabs: *then I graduate college, then I get a job, then I get married, then I have some kids, and then . . .*

So many decisions. So much pressure. It was all too much, too fast. She wanted to enjoy her final year at Thompson Point High, and now it felt like the compounding force of the future was about to crush her.

Sabrina parked her car in the student lot. Another one of her mom's phrases flashed through her mind like an unexpected picture being taken.

The future comes one day at a time.

She nodded, acknowledging the advice and exhaling slowly before grabbing her backpack and opening the door.

One day at a time, she reminded herself. And then, with her bag slung on her shoulders and her head held high, she made her way toward the school building. With each step, she repeated the new mantra she had concocted prior to leaving her house. She wanted to believe it. To have it wash over her.

New face, new outlook, new spirit.
New face, new outlook, new spirit.

Chapter 3

"Sabrina!? Is that you!?"

Rachel's jaw hung open as Sabrina strode down the hallway.

"Wow! You look . . ."

"Fierce?" Sabrina offered.

"Different!" Rachel said.

"I was really hoping you would say fierce." Sabrina laughed.

Rachel eyed her up and down. "Twirl for me."

Sabrina obeyed, her skirt sashaying, before she struck a pose like some fashion model. Joining in on the charade, Rachel put her hands up to her face and pretended to snap pictures.

"Okay," she directed, "if you *really* want to be fierce, then you need to show me! Give me a roar!"

Sabrina raised her hands, her fingers bent like razor-sharp claws. Channeling the energy of the lioness, she emitted a roar that quickly lost its bravado. She stumbled forward, all ferocity gone, and fell into Rachel's arms in a fit of laughter.

"That wasn't *quite* what I was looking for," Rachel said, chuckling equally as much.

"I'll work on it."

They parted, and Rachel looked deeply into Sabrina's jade-colored eyes. "Really, though, I think your new look is great. I just wish you'd told me! I totally would have joined you and done something drastic. I feel left out!"

Sabrina was surprised she'd been able to keep it a secret this long. Normally, she was chomping at the bit to spill any secrets or gossip to Rachel. They called each other nearly every day and hung out just as often.

"I just . . . I needed to do it for myself. I felt, like, if I told you, I might not go through with it. Are you mad?"

"Not at all! But we *could* have done it together! I could use a bit of an update myself." Rachel pushed her blonde bangs off to the side, away from her forehead. A pink scrunchie held the rest of her hair back in a loose, bouncing ponytail. She scrunched her nose and sighed. "Why didn't I think of that? It *is* our senior year, after all. I should have made a statement! Something bold! Something that showed I'm a hip, modern woman of the '90s!"

"You're seventeen," Sabrina snickered. "You *are* pretty hip, but you're not quite a *woman* just yet!"

Before Rachel could respond further, a voice cut through the crowded hallway.

"Hey! What'd you do with my girlfriend?"

Christopher.

Sabrina smirked, curious as to what he would think of her new look. She shifted her gaze in his direction, watching as he strode coolly down the hallway, sunglasses still on with his varsity jacket on display, and awaited his reaction.

Christopher approached, slowly at first, like a predator silently stalking through dense brush. He stroked his chin as if trying to find the meaning in a strange piece of art. Then, after a moment of careful contemplation, he lowered his sunglasses, cracked a smile, and leaned in to plant a kiss on her lips.

He pulled away and tugged on the lioness charm snugged against her throat. "*Whoa*, Sabrina! Can you even breathe with this thing on? If you wanted me to choke you, all you had to do was ask!"

"Christopher!" Sabrina shoved him playfully.

"That's not her kink," Rachel interjected.

"*Oh*, yeah?" Christopher replied, his eyebrows raised with intrigue. "Well, what is it then? I'd love to know! I bet she's into something *really wild*."

"I'll never tell." Rachel mimed zipping her lips and tossing an invisible key over her shoulder.

Sabrina's cheeks blushed a deep shade of crimson. She turned, mouth frozen open in surprise, and lightly pushed Rachel. "What makes you think *you* know what my kink is!?"

"*Oh*, come on," Rachel retorted. "We all know your true kink is getting straight A's!"

"It is not!"

"It's okay, babe. Being smart is *hot*!" He came in for another kiss, but Sabrina swatted him away.

"That's enough from you for now," she said. Christopher took a step back and ran his hands through his thick, golden hair. There was a hint of hurt that shimmered across his face. He slid his sunglasses back into place. He really was handsome, Sabrina couldn't deny that. Almost like a model, with his chiseled chin, ocean eyes, and messy hair, unkempt in a way that was difficult to tell if it was purposefully styled or naturally wild. Of course, Sabrina *knew* it was the latter. Christopher was graced with the charisma and confidence to get out of bed and not even have to look in a mirror. He didn't even own a hairbrush! She was drawn to him physically, but sometimes the things he said made her pause.

On the football field, his prowess was unmatched. She loved watching him play. Loved cheering him on from the sidelines as she waved her pom poms above her head. On paper, it made perfect sense: the Thompson Point Tigers head cheerleader and star football player. But intellectually, Christopher was a bit... lacking. It wasn't that Sabrina didn't *like* him — she did — she just couldn't help but wonder what would happen once the graduation horn sounded and the future, that looming, heavy thing that seemed poised to destroy her, began to unfurl.

One day at a time. Again, her mom's voice barged in unsolicited. Still, though unwanted, it felt needed.

"Did you hear about Mrs. Pike?"

Rachel's question pulled Sabrina back to reality.

"Did I hear about who?"

"Mrs. Pike! I heard she's coming back this year," Rachel said.

"*Oh*, yeah," Sabrina replied. "She's been gone for a couple years now. What happened to her again?"

"Honestly... I don't know," Rachel answered. "I've only heard rumors."

"*I* heard her husband left her for a younger woman," Christopher butted in.

"From who?" Sabrina narrowed her eyes at him incredulously.

"You know . . . *around*. Not one specific person. Just what I've heard, that's all."

"But would that really warrant a two-year absence? Like, would you really leave your job for that long out of heartbreak?" Sabrina asked, though not to either of them in particular.

"I think it's definitely possible," Rachel said with a shrug. "What if that *is* what happened, and it pushed her over the edge? What if she's been in the loony bin this whole time? Finding out your husband is leaving you for someone younger and prettier? That could drive anyone crazy."

"I suppose," Sabrina said with a nod. "What other rumors have you heard?"

"*Oh*, all kinds of things . . ." Rachel bit her bottom lip, pausing for a moment to think. "That she was caring for her sick mother . . . that she just moved away to teach somewhere else for a while . . . that she tried to commit suicide . . ."

"What?" Sabrina interrupted. "Mrs. Pike tried to commit suicide? C'mon now! Are we talking about the same Mrs. Pike who taught our freshman year health class? The same teacher who put together the Thompson Point Olympic Games? The same teacher who started the positivity club? Remember the Smile Squad?"

"Yes, *that* Mrs. Pike. But it's all just rumors. Nobody really knows why she left," Rachel said.

Christopher smirked, pointing down the hallway behind Sabrina. "If you want to know so bad, why not ask her yourself?"

"*Huh?*"

Sabrina whirled around to see Mrs. Pike strolling

in their direction. Almost instantly, she could tell something was different. *Off*.

Her black hair, which fell past her waist, the last Sabrina could remember, was now cut above her shoulders. A bright smile was pasted across her cheeks, pushing through the weathered lines the past few years had forged across her face. There was a bounce in her step, a cheery exuberance that emanated from her movements.

Still, there was something uncanny about it all, something Sabrina couldn't quite place. Maybe it was just the rumors swirling in her head; she wasn't sure.

"Hey! Mrs. Pike!" Rachel greeted her as she approached.

For a split second, she winced, as though she'd gotten a splinter or been bitten by a mosquito. "*Oh*, it's *Ms*. Pike now," she corrected.

"*Ah*," Rachel said, her cheeks now glowing red. "I'm sorry about that. Well, good morning, Ms. Pike."

"Good morning."

"How have you been?" Christopher asked, pulling his sunglasses off and tucking them into the breast pocket of his jacket.

Ms. Pike eyed him quickly, ignoring his question entirely before turning her attention to Sabrina. Her eyes seemed to brighten, and her lips widened into something worthy of representing the Smile Squad.

"Good morning, *Sabrina*! So nice to see you," she said.

"Hi, Ms. Pike," Sabrina greeted with a wave, suddenly feeling awkward.

"I hope you have a lovely day," Ms. Pike offered, beaming one final flash of her smile before continuing. The three of them watched her round the corner toward the teacher's lounge.

Rachel and Christopher were both wide-eyed with confusion.

"What was *that* all about!?" Rachel asked.

"Yeah," Christopher agreed. "*Ms. Pike*? So her husband *did* leave her!"

"Not that! I was talking about not only the way she straight-up ignored you, but also the way she looked at Sabrina and used her name directly. What the heck was that about?"

"I don't know," Sabrina said, shaking her head. "I mean, it's not like I was *close* to her when she did teach here."

Before they could discuss any more, the bell rang, signaling the true start to senior year. With the mystery still thick between them, the trio hurried off to their respective homerooms.

Chapter 4

So far, Sabrina's day was going well. She was pleasantly surprised to discover Rachel was in her first-period calculus class. She was grateful, too, because they had Mr. Lewis, who was notorious for being strict and doling out extremely difficult tests. He'd even assigned homework on the first day! At least they could suffer together.

Second-period English was difficult to navigate, being all the way on the other side of the school. Thankfully, she knew the layout of the building well and was able to cut through the center courtyard to shave a minute off her route to the south wing. Gym, which had always been one of her favorite classes, was up next. Instead of squeaking their sneakers across the gymnasium floor, Mr. Demaris had corralled them outside at the clay courts by the student parking lot to learn the basics of tennis.

It was her fourth-period class Sabrina was dreading most. She sat on a bench in the locker room, sighing as she stared at the class schedule in her hands.

**PERIOD 4: HEALTH - MS. PIKE
EAST WING - ROOM 14**

Sabrina couldn't shake the strangeness she'd felt around Ms. Pike that morning. It was all of it: the cheerfulness in her walk, her spreading smile, the way she'd coldly disregarded Christopher, and how she'd addressed her by name. How come she hadn't greeted Rachel that way? Why had she acted as if Christopher wasn't even there?

Am I overthinking things? Sabrina wondered. *Am I focusing on the rumors too much? I mean, I don't even know the real reason for her absence. Obviously, her husband is out of the picture now; otherwise, she wouldn't have corrected Rachel so quickly. But is that it? Her husband left her? Or maybe she did try to commit suicide afterward? Ah, maybe I am putting too much mental energy into this. I should just mind my business. That's what Mom would say.*

A warning bell cried out, indicating the next period would begin in two minutes. Sabrina sprang up from the bench, folding up her schedule and tucking it into a side pocket on her backpack. Reluctantly, she hurried along to the east wing. She certainly didn't want to be late to the class and draw more attention to herself.

On time is the best time to keep.

As Sabrina increased her pace, breaking into a full-on jog down the hallways, she wondered how long her mom's advice would continue to play out in her head. Had all those phrases been hammered so deeply over the years they were now a permanent fixture of her brain? Was her mom's voice a spirit destined to haunt her head forever? She hoped not.

Sabrina skidded through the doorway of the classroom just as the bell rang and plopped down in the first empty seat she saw.

She gasped as someone tapped her shoulder from behind.

"Since when are you almost late?" Someone whispered with a chuckle.

Sabrina knew that voice. She whipped around with a smile. "Starting today, Christopher. This is the new me. Better get used to it." She playfully poked his chest.

"Feisty, feisty, me likey," Christopher replied, a grin stretching across his face.

Sabrina faced forward, clutching the lioness charm between her left thumb and forefinger.

She was glad to have Christopher there. She hoped the weirdness with Ms. Pike was just a fluke thing, but either way, it was comforting to know he was right there behind her and she wouldn't be totally alone.

She stole a quick glance around the room, curious as to who else was in the class. There were some familiar faces. She waved at Fern Wilton and Danielle Proctor, who were junior cheerleaders. She noticed Billy Palmer and Donald Finch, Christopher's football buddies. As her sweep came to an end, she locked eyes with Gina Applegate and groaned.

Gina glared at her, eyes gleaming like twin daggers ready to puncture. They used to be friendly, but when Sabrina was chosen for head cheerleader over her, she absolutely flipped. Since then, she tried to make things as difficult as possible whenever given the chance. Gina also had a massive crush on Christopher. At least, that's what it seemed like to Sabrina with the way she gave him goo-goo eyes and batted her lashes whenever he was in her vicinity.

Just wonderful, she thought with an eyeroll. *Gina and Ms. Pike! How much more uncomfortable can this period get?*

She let go of the lioness charm and zipped her focus back to the front of the room.

She screamed. Ms. Pike was inches from her desk, staring with her wide eyes and sparkling smile.

"May I begin now, Ms. Quinn?" she asked.

Sabrina nodded, sinking into her seat in embarrassment.

"Wow," Christopher whispered from behind. "Almost late for class *and* not paying attention. You really are a new beast."

"Shut it," Sabrina shot back as quietly as possible.

"I like it," he said.

Ms. Pike took her position at the front of the room, arms behind her back, rocking gently on her heels. She cleared her throat, maintaining her eerie smile, and the noise in the room ceased. Sabrina straightened her spine and sat tall, hands clasped together on her desk, ready to listen and hopefully keep Ms. Pike's attention *away* from her.

"Good morning, everyone. Some of you I recognize from years prior when I used to teach here." Sabrina didn't like that Ms. Pike stared directly at *her* when she said that. "There are also some unfamiliar faces, but for those both new and old, I'm Ms. Pike, and I'll be teaching your health class. The topic for this semester is safe sex and young parenting guidelines. *Obviously*, abstinence is the best and most effective way to prevent an unwanted pregnancy, but that doesn't always happen with teenagers now, does it?"

"Just get an abortion," Billy snickered, high-fiving Donald.

"Excuse me!?" Ms. Pike screeched. Her entire demeanor changed instantly, shifting to something feral and unhinged in a *snap*. She stormed over and pounded her fists atop his desk. "*What* did you say?"

Billy, eyes fully opened with his face frozen in shock, said nothing. Donald attempted to shrink in his seat, hoping to somehow avoid her wrath.

"Say it again!" Ms. Pike demanded.

Sabrina looked on with the rest of the class, stunned at Ms. Pike's outburst, and eager to see what would happen next.

"Just . . . get an *abortion*?" Billy finally spat out.

Ms. Pike's eyes flared with a rageful intensity. Her smile had completely melted away. Now her lips curled back, revealing teeth that looked ready to gnash Billy's head right off his neck. Spit flew from the corners of her mouth.

What is happening? Sabrina wondered, stunned at what was unfolding. It had been so quick, like a flash of lightning. Honestly, it was pretty terrifying. She was just glad it was someone else on the receiving end instead of her.

"*Every* baby deserves to be born! Do you hear me!? *Every baby!*" Ms. Pike fired, her finger pointed in Billy's face. "Do you know how many people out there can't even have babies? Do you realize what some people would do just to have a baby to call their own? *Anything*. You sit there and make a joke like that, as if it's something as simple as returning a videotape! *Abortion?* The only thing getting aborted around here is you from my classroom! NOW GET OUT!"

Without another word, Billy stood and exited the room. The class remained hushed. Ms. Pike then turned to face Donald, who looked away like a dog that had peed on the rug.

"You too, mister. BEAT IT!"

Christopher had to stifle a laugh as he watched Donald practically melt out of his chair and shimmy his way past Ms. Pike and her monstrous glare.

Wow, that really struck a nerve! Sabrina thought, trying to keep a straight face. *She went absolutely ballistic! Is that her secret? Did she have to get an abortion?*

Without moving any other part of her body, Sabrina darted her eyes up at the clock and noticed class was already almost over. In ten minutes, she'd be able to scurry off to lunch and be far away from Ms. Pike and Gina.

"My sincerest apologies," Ms. Pike said as she closed her eyes to collect herself. She brushed off her clothes, as if she were dirty, then looked out at the class once more. Her entire face relaxed and returned to normal, or as normal as this new version of herself could be. Her lips stretched back into a warm smile, and her eyes glistened gently. It was like she had momentarily swapped bodies with someone . . . or *something*. "Now, where were we?"

"Abstinence," Christopher offered.

Ms. Pike nodded, again without fully acknowledging him. Instead, she walked behind her desk and pulled something out from one of the drawers. Then she pivoted to face the students, using the desk as a barrier, and held it up for all to see.

Sabrina shifted back in her seat with surprise at the soft, fleshy thing Ms. Pike held up high.
Is that ... a baby!?

Chapter 5

"Is that a baby?" Sabrina unintentionally blurted out loud.

"*This*," Ms. Pike answered, gently rubbing its bald head, "is the class project. It is a lifelike, battery-operated baby doll, meant to simulate life with a newborn. It does all the things a real baby does."

Ms. Pike pushed some sort of button on the baby's back, and its eyes fluttered open. Sabrina couldn't believe how *real* it looked: the way its chubby legs dangled, to its thick thighs squeezed through the leg holes of its diaper, to its pink cherub cheeks and its now opened eyes, not quite blue or brown but something in-between, that seemed to scan the room with wonder and curiosity. It didn't look like any doll she had ever seen. Certainly not the flimsy, cotton-stuffed ones with hard, plastic heads she had carried around and had tea parties with as a child. This looked *alive*, as though Ms. Pike had snatched it from the local birthing ward on her way to school that morning.

"It cries, it wets its diaper, it drinks a bottle, it closes its eyes to go to sleep," Ms. Pike continued. "In a few weeks, once we've gone over the basics of this course, you will each be taking the baby for a two-week period. You will bring it home and then back to school with you. You will be responsible for the care of this baby. If it dies . . ."

"Dies? It's a doll!" someone from the back of the class shouted. Sabrina wasn't sure who exactly, but it was a boy's voice.

"You are correct, but when it is assigned to you, I expect you will treat it as a living thing. Just like a regular baby, if you neglect it, it *will* die. Everything is recorded by an internal device." Ms. Pike softly tapped the baby's chest to demonstrate this.

"If you ignore its cries, I will know. If you don't change its diaper, I will know. And, if the baby dies, I will know, and you will fail this class. I don't want to fail anyone. I'm not asking for perfection — there is no such thing as the perfect parent, but I want *commitment*. I want you to gain a new perspective. To truly realize and appreciate all that goes into raising a baby. The sacrifice and selflessness that it requires. Maybe, *just maybe*, you will think twice about all I will teach you in this course."

A collective groan whined forth from some of the boys in the back of the classroom. Internally, Sabrina joined in with them. Changing diapers and bottle feeding a doll as if it were a real baby . . . Not exactly the kinds of things she had on her senior year to-do list, that's for sure.

Gina's hand shot up. She wiggled her fingers in the air impatiently. Ms. Pike acknowledged her with a nod.

"Well, I'm just, like, wondering, what about all the other stuff we have going on? Like, I have cheering practices and the homecoming game coming up, and I also have choir, and it's just, like . . . *a lot*."

"The school administration approved this assignment. Everyone, from your other teachers to coaches, knows you will each be caring for the baby for a two-week period. But even so, that just further proves the point of this. What *would* you do if this wasn't a baby doll? How would you manage your schoolwork, your cheering practice, your choir rehearsals, your social engagements, *and* care for a baby?"

Gina sighed. "This is totally not fair. It's our senior year!"

"Is it fair to the babies born from teenage lust? Or even worse, *terminated* because of it?"

Gina didn't answer. Instead, she slumped in her seat, arms crossed, and pouted.

Christopher tapped Sabrina on the shoulder. "Hey, looks like we're gonna have a baby."

"No," Sabrina corrected with a shake of her head, "*I'm* going to have the baby, and then *you're* going to have your turn. I don't recall Ms. Pike saying it was a group project."

Christopher laughed. "Yeah, well, it should be. I mean, what, this baby just has all single parents?"

"I think that's the point of it all," Sabrina said, grinning. "We're supposed to see the struggle of parenting. And here I thought my senior year was going to be all football games and parties, not changing diapers and feeding bottles."

"It's gonna be a long two weeks, that's for sure. But you'll help me, right? I can't handle a baby all alone!"

"You handle yourself just fine," Sabrina said with a snort.

"*Very funny*," Christopher replied in a low, comical tone.

Sabrina had never been happier to hear the bell as it expelled its annoying chime into the air. She rushed up from her seat and flung her backpack onto her shoulders, but before she could scoot past her desk, Gina was there blocking her way.

"Can I help you?" Sabrina asked. She felt Christopher's presence behind her, like a shadowed bodyguard. And while she appreciated the gesture, it certainly wasn't helping to bolster her tougher image.

"Just wanted to say that I, like, can't wait to see what you've cooked up for our cheer routine this year. I'm sure it's gonna be, like, totally rad." Gina flashed the pearliest smile she could muster. If this were the savanna, Sabrina would have slashed her claws right across Gina's taunting, fake grin.

"I guess you'll just have to see at practice. Just make sure you can keep up with the *head* cheerleader." Sabrina gave a wink that soured Gina's lips into a scowl almost instantly.

"You're lucky you were, like, already elected head cheerleader, because if you went in there with *this* look?" Gina reached forward and flicked the lioness charm, pulling her hand away before Sabrina could retaliate. "You would have *never* been picked. See you in the gymnasium, *Sabrina*."

"Are we talking nicely, girls? Is there anything we need to discuss?"

Sabrina looked up to see Ms. Pike looming behind Gina, her face shining like an overly bright sun. Any remnants of the monster from earlier were long gone.

"No," Gina replied, trying to mask her scowl. She turned and marched stiffly out of the room.

"Wonderful," Ms. Pike said. She was still holding onto the baby doll, grasping it around its belly. Sabrina couldn't help but stare at its soft flesh up close, amazed by its realness, its authenticity.

Was it warm to the touch? What material do they use to make it seem like skin? How much does a doll like that cost?

A light weight pressed into Sabrina's back. It was Christopher, ushering her out of the classroom.

"Have a great rest of your day, Sabrina," Ms. Pike said.

Instinctively, Sabrina stopped suddenly to turn and say something in return. Christopher nearly tripped over her, his hand still on the small of her back, surprised by her unexpected halt.

But Sabrina never got to say anything. The words were stolen from her lips. It was the baby doll that caught her attention again. Only this time, it *winked* at her, shutting one of its blueish-hazel eyes before opening up once more.

Chapter 6

All eyes were on Sabrina as she stood before the cheerleading team. Her first day of senior year was *almost* over. She just had to get through cheering practice. Hopefully, Gina would ease the brakes on being such a witch, but Sabrina didn't hold her breath. That was okay, though; *she* was the head cheerleader, and here, in the gymnasium, she ran the show.

Sabrina eyed the girls as they stood in formation, hands on their hips, clutching their poms poms at their sides. Every girl was in uniform, a blue and yellow bodyliner with the words "Thompson Point" in varsity font and a pleated skirt matching the school colors.

"I'm going to run through the cheer again," Sabrina said. "Remember the positions I showed you. The chant is *'TIGERS, let's hear you roar, TIGERS, you want some more? TIGERS, lay that team to rest, TIGERS, we are the best! T-I-G-E-R-S, we go for the gold and play to impress. T-I-G-E-R-S, we'll rip you apart and make you a mess. Go, Tigers!'* Can we do it?"

Gina chomped on a large wad of gum and rolled her eyes up into the back of her skull. "Yeah," she answered, blowing a huge pink bubble and then popping it, "we *got it*."

"Well, let's see it then," Sabrina replied with a smirk. "Stacy, I want you to swap places with Laura. If you feel yourself falling behind, just watch the others around you. This is only practice, but we *need* to nail this for the pep rally and the homecoming game! Remember, pom poms high, shake them with spirit and smile, smile, smile!"

Gina scoffed, but still followed directions and took her place. Sabrina was about to count them in when she happened to look up and noticed Lawrence sitting on the bleachers, watching intently.

What is he doing here? Sabrina wondered. It wasn't necessarily weird to have people hang around and watch them practice. Oftentimes, freshman girls interested in trying out for the team would stay and observe. Or certain cheerleaders' boyfriends would cluster around the gymnasium to show support. But none of those things applied to Lawrence. *Is he here to watch me?*

"*Oh*, mighty and fearless leader, are you planning to start us off sometime today?" Gina's callous tone hooked into Sabrina, pulling her back to the practice at hand.

"*Huh? Oh* yeah, sorry, girls." Sabrina shook her head and refocused her brain. *Just pretend he's not even here.* "Let's take it from the top. Ready? One, two, three, GO!"

Still, despite her best efforts, Sabrina found it difficult to keep her attention on her team. Just knowing Lawrence was there really threw her off. She peered over her shoulder and, for a second, they locked eyes. Lawrence gave a half-smile, but Sabrina whisked her head back around just as quickly. Her stomach tightened with nerves.

Why is he here!? Why today, during our first official practice? He's lucky Christopher isn't here; otherwise, he might be leaving the school with a few less teeth. Or at the very least, a bloody nose.

Sabrina tried to concentrate on her team as they worked through the routine. Everything was a blur. She heard the rustling of the pom poms as the girls shook them and saw the spins and twirls of their blue and yellow uniforms, but everything felt distant. Like she was banished to purgatory, lost in some other realm, watching from afar.

Someone screamed, and a loud crash thundered through the gymnasium. Sabrina snapped back to reality to find Laura Summers, the newest recruit, on the floor in tears, holding her knee and rocking back and forth.

"*Hellllooo*, head cheerleader! Are you, like, gonna pay attention and coach us or not?" Gina asked, hands on her hips, her voice brimming with sarcasm and as prickly as a thorn bush.

Sabrina ignored Gina and rushed over to inspect Laura's injuries.

"Are you okay? What happened?"

"It's ... my knee ... It hurts so bad!" Laura sniffled and wiped her eyes, fighting against another onrush of tears. "I took a wrong step and bumped into Gina and ... and ... she *pushed* me ..."

"She what!?" Sabrina shrieked, immediately swiveling her head to glare at Gina.

"*Me?*" Gina replied, wide-eyed with disbelief at the

accusation. "Please. I was only, like, trying to keep this whole team together while our *supposed* head cheerleader was off in space!"

"I wasn't off in space, I was . . ." Sabrina glanced toward the bleachers, but Lawrence was gone.

When did he leave?

Sabrina sighed. "Okay, listen, practice is over for today. We will reconvene tomorrow right after school. Gina, *you* can help me escort Laura to the nurse's office. The rest of you, have a good night and practice reciting the cheer!"

"Why should *I* have to help?"

"Because *I* said so!" Sabrina felt the lioness moving through her when she said it. Gina seemed to pick up on that and, instead of another comeback, silently helped Laura to her feet. Sabrina stepped in, placing Laura's other arm over her shoulder to help brace her, and together they guided her to the school nurse.

"Thank you, Sabrina," Laura said.

"No problem. All right, here we are. Let's place her down gently on the chair, and I'll talk to Mrs. Ward."

Gina kept quiet and helped lower Laura onto the chair in the waiting area, then, without even a good-bye or apology, slipped off into the hallway and disappeared.

"*Pffft*, typical Gina," Sabrina said, shaking her head.

Laura winced and grabbed at her knee again.

Mrs. Ward poked her head out from her office. "What do we have here?"

"She fell and hurt her knee, not sure how bad it is," Sabrina explained.

Mrs. Ward bent down to inspect Laura's injury.

"Definitely swollen for sure. I'll get you an ice pack to reduce the swelling, and we'll call your parents."

"I'm so sorry, Laura," Sabrina offered. She rubbed her shoulder. Mrs. Ward returned from her office with an ice pack a moment later and gave it to Laura.

"Just hold that in place, and I'll get your parents on the line."

Laura nodded, placing the cold bag on her knee.

"I'll check on you tomorrow, okay?" Sabrina said.

Laura nodded. "Thanks again. I think I'll be okay. It feels better already with the ice pack."

Sabrina waved and exited into the hallway. Now that all the commotion was over, she realized she had to go pee really badly. The nearest bathroom was only a few doors down and to the left. She sprinted to it, suddenly aware of how empty the school was and how loud her footsteps echoed across the halls.

Turning the corner, she put her gears into overdrive, dashing to the bathroom with increased intensity. Her thighs trembled. She *really* had to go now. In another minute, her body was going to let go. She was still in her cheering skirt. It would soak through her underwear and run down her legs. Not exactly the way she wanted to end her first day of senior year.

Almost there! C'mon, go, go, go!

She yanked on the door, but it wouldn't budge. That was when she noticed the sign:

CLOSED FOR MAINTENANCE

No! She pounded her fist on the door in equal parts frustration and in the hopes the janitor, or *anyone*, might open up and let her in. No such luck. Aside from the scuffling of her feet as she danced in place to keep from wetting herself, the hallway was thick with silence.

What about the boys' room? Sabrina pulled on the door with the same results. Both bathrooms were locked. She knocked, even though she knew no one would answer.

"Hello? Is anyone in there? It's an emergency! Please, *please*, open up!"

The next bathroom she could think of was all the way in the south wing. She'd never make it.

Wait a minute! The idea sprang into her head like a gift from the heavens. *The basement! There's a bathroom down in the basement by the janitor's office.*

Still hopping up and down as though her shoes were fitted with springs, Sabrina hurried toward the basement stairwell at the end of the hall. She bounded down, skipping multiple steps, desperate to reach the bathroom before her bladder burst.

It was dark *and* quiet in the basement. Shadows clung to the cool, brick walls. Sabrina tried to reach back into her memories for the quickest route to the bathroom. She'd only been down there once, last year, when the janitor was tied up with something, and someone had spilled an entire cooler of Gatorade in the gymnasium. Sabrina had taken it upon herself to go and find a mop and bucket.

The lights had been brighter then. And she wasn't in a race with her own body. Aside from a few dim, flickering bulbs spaced far apart, Sabrina was feeling her way through the darkness, running her fingers along the brick walls as a guide.

Her steps were bouncy, continuing the dance she had started in the hallway. She took short, labored breaths as she talked her way through. "Okay, we turn right here, and the janitor's office should be up ahead. The bathroom was right across from it. Just keep going. Almost there. Hold it. Hold it. *Please*, just hold it."

Now her legs were trembling. Her bladder was at its absolute limit. Her stomach squeezed itself. A few drips trickled out. Sabrina could feel the small, wet puddle forming in her underwear.

I'm not going to make it!

Then she saw it, appearing in a flash from one of the lights above, the sacred door she'd been searching for. It was within her reach. She soldiered on, her entire body shaking, and pushed the door open.

Sabrina had never been so excited to be in a school bathroom before. A long, fluorescent light twinkled above, maintaining the same dim atmosphere as the rest of the basement. But it was enough. She could see the stalls and made her way into the nearest one, shutting the door, ripping her underwear down to her knees, and plopping down onto the toilet.

The relief was instant and felt so good, Sabrina thought she might cry. Her legs began to relax and loosen once more. She hunched forward on the toilet and buried her face in her hands. It was such a welcome feeling that at first, she hardly noticed or heard the approaching footsteps coming toward the bathroom.

Chapter 7

The light went out, plunging the bathroom into total blackness. Sabrina couldn't ignore the footsteps any longer. Whoever it was, they were now in the room with her.

Clack, clack, clack.

Quickly, Sabrina slid her underwear back up but remained in the stall. It was so dark she could hardly see her hand in front of her face.

"Ha-ha, very funny," she called out. "Is that you, Gina? Did you follow me down here? You can turn the light back on now."

The footsteps stopped outside of her stall. Her question went unanswered.

"Give it a rest, will you? When are you going to let it go? It's not *my* fault you weren't picked for head cheerleader. We used to be friends, remember that?"

The intruder said nothing. Sabrina didn't hear any more footsteps, but she also couldn't tell if someone was still standing on the other side of the door. She had the same amount of visibility as closing her eyes.

"Hello? Are you going to answer me? I know it's you, Gina. You can stop with the games. I was just trying to pee. Turn on the light and leave me alone.

You're going to be really sorry at practice tomorrow when I make you do conditioning the entire time."

Still no answer. The silence settled around Sabrina like an unwanted hug.

Was it not Gina? She wondered. *Surely, she would have made some snide remark by now. Or cackled or done something... right?*

The stall door rattled lightly, like a normal inspection someone might do to see if the toilet was occupied. Sabrina gritted her teeth in annoyance.

"Whoever it is, you'd better stop now! Whatever game you think you're playing? Cut it out!"

The door shook again, harder this time. The sensation reverberated throughout the entire stall. Sabrina scooted back slightly atop the toilet, her aggravation beginning to crumble into fear.

Who could it be? Was it Lawrence? Had he disappeared from the gymnasium only to secretly follow her? No one knew she was down here. He could do anything...

"Is that you, Lawrence?" she called out. She tried to hide the shakiness in her voice and pulled at the charm, hoping to gather more of its strength. The quiet was really getting to her. That and the thought of someone standing on the other side of the door, drenched in darkness, waiting.

"Listen, Lawrence, if it is you, you'd *better* get out of here. I don't know what your fascination with me is, but you can't follow me around, *especially* into the bathroom. I'm only going to say it one more time: turn the lights back on before I start screaming for help."

Instead of a reply to her statement, Sabrina heard

something else. A soft, breathy whisper that sang to her.

"Hush little baby, don't say a word, mommy's gonna buy you a mockingbird..."

The blood iced over in Sabrina's veins. She huddled on top of the toilet, tucking her knees into her chest and hugging them tight. Fear quaked through her body in quivering waves.

At least I remembered to lock the door before I peed myself.

Just as she thought that, the door rumbled from a brute force slam. Whatever the intruder was using, their shoulder or some kind of weapon, they pounded into the door again. And again. A relentless volley of pummeling blows.

"What do you want!?" she screamed. "Go away! This isn't funny anymore!"

BOOM! BOOM! BOOM!

The door began to buckle. Sabrina could hear wood splintering in the shadows. The little lock wasn't going to stop anything. Another hit smashed into the door, loosening some of the screws in the hinges and sending them bouncing across the floor.

All Sabrina could do was listen and wait. There was nowhere for her to go. She was trapped in the stall. The stalker had her right where they wanted her. No one would hear her screams. By now, the school had to have been mostly emptied out.

"...and if that mockingbird don't sing, mommy's gonna buy you a diamond ring..."

Sabrina let out a bloodcurdling scream and raised her arms to shield her face as pieces of the door flew across the stall like shrapnel.

What are they using, a hammer!? Why are they doing this!?

One more swift and powerful hit was enough to break the lock. The door swung open, banging into the side of the stall. Sabrina screamed into the darkness. She never saw the hand reach in. She had no idea what was happening until she felt the grip of fingers wrap around one of her legs and was wrenched off the toilet.

She tried to grab hold of the lid but wasn't quick enough. With the same strength used to break down the door, Sabrina was pulled from the stall and out onto the floor of the bathroom. A stinging, chemical aroma fizzled up into her nostrils. Her skin was wet and sticky. Had the janitor recently cleaned the floor, or was it something else?

There was no time to ponder. The mysterious attacker grabbed Sabrina by the armpits and pulled her to her feet. They held her from behind, with one gloved hand over her lips. She could taste the leather as it mixed with the spit in her mouth. Hot tears fell from her eyes. She was too terrified to move, let alone scream anymore.

Something cold and sharp ran along her neck. Sabrina gulped and clenched her eyes shut even though she was already wrapped in a world of darkness. Part of her thought that maybe if she closed them, this wouldn't be real. That maybe this was nothing more than the nightmarish tendrils of an afternoon nap. A culmination of exhaustion and the lingering thoughts in her head from the summer stalker.

It didn't help. This was *real*. This person, this

intruder, wasn't some shadow in her bushes or a phantom of her imagination. They were *here*, down in the basement of the school, pressed against her, running what she could only surmise was a knife up and down her neck. They pressed the tip of the blade into her skin playfully, not drawing blood but just enough to show they could if they wanted to.

"*. . . and if that diamond ring turns to brass, mommy's gonna buy you a looking glass . . .*"

The song floated into her ears like a soft haunting, like a ghost made of nothing but a silky sheet. It nestled into her brain as the tears continued to slowly leak from her tightly shut eyelids. The gloved grip tightened on her face. The leather smell overwhelmed her. Sabrina nearly gagged, using every ounce of mental power she had left to keep from doing so. Her head felt light and airy, like she could pass out at any second.

The knife slipped beneath the velvet collar of her choker necklace. She felt the pressure from the blade and then a release. The stalker's other hand withdrew from her mouth, grabbing hold of the charm and ripping the accessory from her neck.

Then she heard a scurry of footsteps leaving the bathroom, echoing into the darkness. Sabrina drew in a deep breath, free of leather, and spit onto the floor. Above, the bulb shimmered back to life, pulsing with a pale, white glow.

Sabrina's eyes slowly adjusted to the returning light. She was alone once more. She turned to look at herself in the mirror. Black lines streaked down her cheeks from the tears ruining her makeup. Turning on the cold water, she lowered her face into the sink, attempting to wash away the dark stains as best as she could.

Almost on impulse, upon lifting her head back up and looking long and hard into the dingy, frosted glass, she reached for the lioness charm, momentarily forgetting it was no longer there. Instead, her fingers touched the bare skin of her neck, then slowly traveled across the imprint left behind by the choker.

Chapter 8

"What happened to your choker by the way? Haven't seen you wear it for a few days now. I thought it was part of your new *identity*," Rachel asked as she shoved a handful of french fries into her mouth. Usually, she was very cognizant of her appearance, especially when cute boys might be nearby, but when it came to the mall food court's french fries, all reservations were off. She liked boys, especially Seth Vansickle, but she liked fries even more. French fries never disappointed her.

"It was..." Sabrina paused. She hadn't told anyone about the incident in the bathroom at school. Not her parents. Not Christopher. Not even Rachel. Frankly, she didn't know *what* to do. The story seemed so crazy, so far-fetched. Who would believe it?

The bathroom stall door had been busted in, so there *was* some evidence, but still, who would believe it was some figure in the shadows whispering lullabies while holding her at knifepoint? The janitor would discover the door eventually, and rowdy teenagers causing some damage to the basement bathroom seemed more plausible. Plus, being head cheerleader *and* class valedictorian, there were already so many eyes on her. Sabrina didn't want that kind of extra attention. She didn't want to suddenly be known as the girl who got attacked in the bathroom. *Those* are the kinds of things that can overshadow your accomplishments. The kinds of things that can become your personality, your entire being.

She shuddered, suddenly drawn right back, feeling the phantom sensation of the knife slowly dragging across her neck. Sabrina gagged as the suffocating aroma of the leather glove returned and the haunting melody of the lullaby played out in her ears.

"It was *what*?" Rachel asked, sucking in a stray fry that was jutting out of her lips like a snaggletooth. "Are you okay?"

"Yeah." Sabrina sighed. "Sorry, there's just been a lot on my mind with school and cheering, and the homecoming festivities. I've been a little . . . out of it."

"Your choker?"

"What?" Sabrina reached up and grazed her neck, half-expecting the necklace to still be there.

"You never finished telling me what happened with it."

"*Oh*, nothing really. It was just a bit tight, so I decided not to wear it anymore."

Around them, the mall bustled with teenage distortion and busy families. Rachel nodded toward a woman swiftly pushing a double stroller past the food court as the two babies inside shrieked. The stress on the poor woman's face was as apparent as a slathering of makeup.

"It's going to suck," Rachel remarked.

"Growing up?"

"No! Ms. Pike's assignment! The baby doll." Rachel laughed and scrounged up the last few fries left on her tray. She continued as she chomped on them: "I mean, growing up might also suck, too, but this baby project is going to *really* suck."

"Yeah, as if we don't already have enough going on during senior year."

"I know! The nerve of that woman! *Gah*, does she not remember what it's like to be a teenager? We should be out having fun and mowing down on fries and kissing boys . . ."

"I think that's the point," Sabrina interrupted with a giggle. "Kissing boys is the first part of the equation."

Rachel stared at her empty tray and sighed, looking completely bummed out. Sabrina wasn't sure if the look was about the project or the fact that she was out of fries. It could have been a combination of both.

"One thing is for sure," Rachel said, perking back up. "You can kiss shopping sprees goodbye! Unless you count buying diapers and formula from the supermarket as retail therapy."

"Definitely *not*," Sabrina agreed.

She pictured the baby doll in her mind with its pudgy, life-like skin and those eyes. Those crystalline hazel spheres staring as if there were life behind them. And then Sabrina recalled that the baby doll had winked at her.

But that's impossible! Or is it? If it could wet itself and cry when it was hungry and shut its eyes to sleep, then was it really that much of a stretch that it could quickly close and open just one of its eyes? No, it's really not. Get ahold of yourself, Sabrina! It's just a baby doll. Even if it looks real, it's not. Why would it blink at you specifically?

Still, even if her imagination was running a bit wild, the fact remained that someone out there *was* stalking her. There was no disputing that fact now. It was no longer a rustle in the bushes or a soft lullaby that could be mistaken for a summer breeze. No, whoever the shadowed intruder was, they had made contact. They had touched her. Held a knife to her throat. Cut the choker right off her neck.

And for what?

That's what continued to linger in Sabrina's brain. Why take the necklace? They could have had their way with her. They could have violated her right there in the darkness. They could have *killed* her. The knife was right there, flush against her flesh. All they had to do was slice her throat open or stab the blade into an artery. But they didn't. They didn't leave a mark. The knife had teased, almost like kisses from Christopher on her neck, but that was it. Just a tease. Or a threat, lingering. A cold reminder that they *could* if they wanted to.

Fear-laced confusion encircled Sabrina like a misty fog. Who could it be? Who wanted it out for her so badly? Gina was the obvious answer, but there's no way she was strong enough to smash open a locked door like that. At least Sabrina didn't think so. She was mean and nasty, that's for sure, but was she capable of borderline *attempted murder*?

And what about the lullabies? If it *was* Gina, then what was that all about? The whispering didn't sound like her, but she might have been changing her voice to sound scary. Did that mean Gina had spent her entire summer plotting and hiding in Sabrina's bushes to sing lullabies to her? And then attack her in one of the school bathrooms?

Lawrence was another possibility. Sure, he was weird, and his incessant staring definitely creeped Sabrina out, but was he really so obsessed with her that it would drive him to kill?

She liked the third option even less: that the stalker was some unknown person with mysterious motives. That they moved in shadow and secrecy. That they could strike at any given moment, and Sabrina would have no idea. It could be *anyone*, and now they had one of her personal objects.

So, the question remained, clogging her head like hair in a shower drain: what could they possibly want her necklace for? Was that all they wanted, or were they going to come back for more?

"*Helllooo*? Sabrina? Are you there?"

Sabrina came to, as if waking from a dream, to find Rachel waving a hand in front of her face.

"*Huh?*"

"I lost you again. Are you sure you're okay?"

"Yeah," Sabrina lied. "Nothing a little ice cream couldn't fix."

"*Ooh!* Now you're talking! C'mon, let's go!"

As they stood and started walking toward the exit doors, Sabrina couldn't help but look around at all the other people patrolling the mall. Anxiety struck her chest with a force equal to that of the stalker's blast against the bathroom stall door. They really could be anywhere. They could even be there now, in the mall, watching and waiting for their next opportune chance to attack. As the automatic doors slid open and the girls stepped out onto the sidewalk in front of the mall, Sabrina couldn't help but feel like her entire world had grown a bit smaller and nothing in it was safe.

Chapter 9

Weeks later, with dozens more cheering practices under her belt, homework beginning to pile up, and the thrumming spirit of the impending homecoming festivities flowing through her, Sabrina had *almost* forgotten about the stalker.

The thought still lingered, obviously. How could it not? It wasn't like she was apt to *forget* the pure terror that had pumped through her veins, or that feeling of pure helplessness as the gloved hand covered her mouth and the sharp blade of the knife danced across her neck.

But since the incident in the bathroom, it was like the stalker had vanished. There'd been no more noises in her bushes at night. No more lullabies whispering through her bedroom windows. And, best of all, no more random attacks.

Sabrina had kept her eye on Gina, but aside from her usual cattiness, none of her behavior was out of the ordinary. It was almost comical in a way, as the days passed on, to think of Gina, prissy little, wished-she-was-head-cheerleader Gina, ducking low in the shadows of her bushes as she softly sang lullabies in the warm summer night air.

At this point, it was hard for Sabrina *not* to burst out laughing anytime she made some snide comment because all she could picture was Gina with her knees in the dirt and leaves stuck in her hair with her hand cupped to her lips as she quietly called out baby songs like "Twinkle, Twinkle, Little Star".

She'd made sure to keep watch on Lawrence, too. He seemed to be keeping with his usual routines as well. They shared history class, but aside from that, Sabrina was only able to get quick glances of him as they passed one another in the hallway or in the lunch line. He still made some appearances in the bleachers at cheering practice, but she didn't let it bother her anymore.

As the gray September days started to grow chillier and the early autumn breeze whipped through the already changing leaves, Sabrina made sure that no matter where she went, she was never alone. She didn't go to the bathroom, walk the halls, or change in the locker room unless *at least* two other people were present. Even though her nerves were easing and she was slipping into a routine she enjoyed, she didn't want to give *anyone* a chance to surprise her or put herself in another situation like that again.

Sabrina kept her fingers crossed, hoping it really was the end of it. She still wanted her choker back. Oftentimes in class or in her room, as she lay on her bed doing homework, her fingers would subconsciously reach toward her neck, and it wasn't until they grazed bare skin instead of the expected lioness charm that the realization would hit like a hard smack across her face. Even if she was thankful that whoever it was had only taken the necklace and not something like a finger—or worse, her life—she couldn't help but feel like a piece of her was missing.

Either way, the homecoming preparations were a much-welcomed distraction. Not only was she head cheerleader, but Sabrina was also part of the festivities committee. To her delight, Rachel had decided to join this year, and everything would've been absolutely perfect if Gina hadn't also signed up. At least they outnumbered her, and there was so much to do—like painting banners, setting up hay bales, carving jack-o'-lanterns, hanging decorations in the gymnasium, preparing the pep rally, and coordinating the homecoming dance—that they didn't have to be around her all that much.

A busy mind keeps wandering thoughts at bay.

It wasn't one of her mom's usual phrases, but it was one that had been offered on a few occasions. It seemed more apt now than ever. The last thing she needed was her mind to spiral, for her thoughts to travel to dark places and drive her insane.

Not only was fall Sabrina's favorite season, but it was her *last* one as a high schooler, and she was determined to enjoy it. She'd worked so hard her entire life; she deserved to relish in all of Thompson Point High's autumnal happenings.

It was *her* job to spread the school spirit. To inspire it within her peers. *She* was the conduit through which the tiger of Thompson Point bared its fangs and showed off its stripes.

It was only now that Sabrina realized how truly fitting it was that a tiger was her school's mascot. A tiger was just as tough and fierce as a lioness and could only help to embolden her further as she channeled its energy for Homecoming and beyond.

This was *her* time.

Feeling bits of both the tiger and the lioness surging within, she vowed to make it the best season she could.

While waiting for Christopher to pick her up and take her to a late-night bonfire, Sabrina sat before her vanity, staring into the mirror and ensuring her makeup and hair were perfect. She cracked a smile as she gently placed a hand on her throat, feeling the phantom energy of the lioness like prickles of static electricity on her fingers.

Outside, she heard a car pull up into her driveway and then the distinctive *beep* from Christopher's horn. Grabbing her purse and slinging it over her shoulder, she gave one last inspection. As a finishing touch, she tucked her hair behind her ears, then flashed a satisfied thumbs-up to her reflection.

This *was* going to be the best Homecoming ever, she was sure of that. The only thing that could possibly stop it was death itself.

Oh, Sabrina, my perfect little vessel.

I didn't mean to scare you. That's the last thing I wanted. But I had to do what I had to do. I hope someday you'll understand.

You deserve the best. Everything on a golden platter. Whatever comforts I can provide going forward, I will, as long as it adheres to the plan, of course.

I will leave you alone now ... for a little while anyway. I'll allow you to breathe for a bit. Let you think I've vanished into the shadows. The first step is complete: a personal object.

The necklace ... It carries your scent. Like sweat and butterflies and lavender. Sometimes I wear it, and I close my eyes and pretend to be you. I try to imagine what it's like to be so ... perfect.

You truly have it all.

How does it feel to move without worry? To exude such beauty and confidence? To wake up every day with a body that hasn't failed you?

I'll never be you, but I will have a part of you.

Sabrina, my darling, my angel, you will bear the light, you will give me what I deserve. What I need.

Enjoy your trips to the mall and the cruises in Christo-

pher's car. Savor his kisses, because they won't be around forever. He won't be around forever. I'll make sure of that.

I am your eternal.

You are the Tree of Life.

The Fountain of Youth.

The Bearer of Fruit.

The most exquisite carrier.

I would do this all for you if I could. I would suffer for you. Absorb all your pain and agony. But I've already tried and failed. It's your time to shine. Your turn to step up to the plate.

The gears are in motion. You only think it's over because I want you to. Everything is according to the plan. There is so much more work to do. But it will be worth it, oh *so worth it.*

You have the most important role of all, Sabrina. You don't know that yet, but you do.

Live it up for now, my perfect vessel. Enjoy the fun with friends because soon, the party will be over . . .

Chapter 10

"Christopher, I'm going to freeze!" Sabrina yelled, noticing his car was in its convertible mode, with the detachable roof section removed.

"It's not *that* chilly!" Christopher shot back. "Besides, I have to get as much use out of the open top as I can before winter comes. Come on, live a little! Kick back and feel the wind in your hair!"

Sighing, Sabrina zipped up her sweatshirt and opened the passenger side door. As she climbed in, she noticed a hump covered with a blanket in the backseat. Curiously, she reached around and pulled up a corner of the cover to find a 12-pack of beer.

"Christopher James!" she cried out with a laugh.

"What!?" he replied, putting both his hands up in protest. "We're going to a *party*, remember?"

"*You* just better hope none of the cops pull you over before we get there. Otherwise, you'll be having a very different kind of party." Sabrina flashed him a cheeky smile and playfully punched his shoulder.

"*Oh*, please," Christopher said, smirking with an air of superiority. "You really think they are going to pull over the star quarterback right before the season kicks off?"

"So confident," Sabrina commented with a roll of her eyes. "Just be careful how big that head of yours inflates. Once we graduate, you won't be the Thompson Point star quarterback anymore."

"You're right," Christopher said with a smirk, his teeth still on full display. "*Then* I'll be the star quarterback for whatever college I end up at."

Sabrina let the conversation stop there. Instead of replying, she buckled herself in to indicate she was ready to go. As she did, she became suddenly aware of a new smell in his car, a minty evergreen that hovered in the air. Looking up, she noticed a dark green tree-shaped air freshener dangling from the bottom of the rearview mirror. The last one Christopher hung there was red and reeked of cinnamon, which got to be a bit much for her. The pine scent was a welcome change.

Christopher put the car in reverse, swerving out of her driveway in a fast, fluid motion. He snickered and shifted the gear into drive, blasting the car off down the street.

You just keep playing with fire, don't you? Sabrina thought, a sliver of her wishing he would get pulled over just to learn a lesson. But a much larger part of her relished his bravado and wild recklessness. There really was something so sexy about his devil-may-care attitude, something Sabrina couldn't place. She just couldn't help but wonder how long it would be until it all caught up with him. One day, the flames were going to burn him.

The wind roared through the open car, rustling their hair and making conversation virtually impossible. Instead, Sabrina tilted her head toward what normally was the window and let the cool night air whip across her face. Christopher cranked the volume dial on the radio. The song that blasted out of the speakers was one Sabrina wasn't familiar with, and though it sounded slightly distorted from the wild wind, the steady, pounding beat of the drums allowed her to follow the rhythm.

"*Ooh!* This is a good one!" Christopher shouted, nodding his head along to the *thud* of the snare drum. "You heard of Nine Inch Nails? Probably not, *huh?*"

Sabrina ignored him, content to stare up at the burgeoning stars as the night rushed past. It wasn't until the vocalist on the song started to sing—or maybe chant was the right word, the voice was soft and breathy—that the hair on the back of her neck began to stand up. It wasn't necessarily *how* they were singing, but *what* they were saying that alarmed her. The words they had used.

Violate.

Penetrate.

A knot formed as the first couple lines of the song wormed through her ears and settled into her stomach. She grabbed hold of the door handle as an anchor, something to keep her steady. She didn't think she was going to throw up, and definitely didn't want to mess up the interior of Christopher's beloved car, but the song . . . the song was doing something to her.

It was all rushing back now. All the thoughts and feelings she'd tried to keep submerged. All the things she'd been trying to forget. The fact that the song had a funky, danceable beat added to its haunting quality. Like something sinister disguised as something fun.

"Help me get away from myself..."

The darkness smiled at her. The cold kiss of the night wind felt like a hundred gloved hands, reaching out to touch her, to run long, leather-clad fingers through her hair. Sabrina wanted to scream. She wanted to crawl out of her skin. To open the door, fall to the pavement, and roll off into the dark expanse of woods by the side of the road. Anything to stop the mounting dread, the growing unease.

"I wanna..." Christopher began to belt along to the chorus.

Squirming in her seat, unable to bear it any longer, Sabrina whipped her hand up and turned the radio off.

"*Hey!* I was listening to that!" Christopher turned to glare at her and accidentally jerked the wheel as he did. He immediately corrected the car, guiding it back onto the road and within the painted lines.

"It was too noisy," Sabrina said, now groping blindly behind her, searching for the covered case of beer in the backseat. She tugged the blanket off and then tore off a side of the cardboard, grabbing the first can her fingers touched. She'd never drunk a beer before, or any alcohol for that matter, but what better time than on the verge of a panic attack under the open top of her boyfriend's car?

"*Whoa!*" Christopher shouted when he heard Sabrina crack the can open. "Weren't you just scolding me for having beer in the car, and now you're just going to start drinking them? If I *did* get pulled over, I'd get in even more trouble for having an open can!"

Sabrina said nothing, bringing the cold can to her lips. She absolutely hated the taste, pausing a moment to force her first gulp down. But the important thing was to forget. To let loose. To have fun. She *had* to drink the rest of the can. It was the only way she was going to get through the party without completely falling apart.

Chapter 11

Most of the Thompson Point citizens were aware of the clearing set deep in the Everly Forest and knew teenagers liked to party there, but it was tucked far enough back that people tended to look the other way, the cops included. Similar to the mentality of *boys will be boys* (a phrase that was not in her mom's repertoire, given that Sabrina was a girl), the general thinking was *teenagers do stupid things. Let them live and learn.*

Christopher guided Sabrina through the wooded trail that led to the spot where the bonfire was being held. Somehow, she'd managed to down three beers before he had parked the car. He was equally impressed and annoyed. She'd kept the drinks down, which he was thankful for, but now she was a dizzy mess, and he was going to have to babysit her. He eased her forward gently, keeping one hand on her shoulders while he cradled the case of beer in his other arm.

Soon, the trail through the dark tangle of trees brought them to the clearing with a makeshift shack and a massive bonfire raging outside of it. Crowds of shadowed teenagers milled about, shouting and cheering. To Sabrina, they were nothing more than blackened shapes. Everything in her eyes was a dance of colors.

"No more drinks for you," Christopher whispered into her ear.

"*Don't tell me...*" Sabrina sassed.

"I *am* telling you," Christopher cut in. "You've already had enough. I have to make sure you are safe."

"*Yo*, Chris!" one of his teammates shouted from the darkness.

"*Yooo!*" Christopher yelled in return, though he wasn't entirely sure who it was.

Sabrina's senses were all off. Her nose wasn't registering the smoky smell of the massive bonfire or the pungent aroma of cheap beer that permeated the air. Her eyes saw only shapes. All details were lost in the flickering shadows cast by the tall flame. She was brimming with gratitude for Christopher. She would have tripped a hundred times over if it weren't for his guiding hands. The world seemed like it was tilted, like she was walking at an angle.

They reached the bonfire, and Christopher sat Sabrina down onto one of the logs on the perimeter. Even though she was seated, she found keeping her balance was just as much of a challenge as walking. The heat from the fire warmed her entire body. For the time being, her dark thoughts and anxiety had receded. At the moment, all she could think about was kissing Christopher. Of their lips pressed together in a passionate embrace just as fiery as the towering flames.

"*Hey, Christopher,*" a sultry voice slithered forth

from the shadows. Even in a stupor, Sabrina recognized it.

Gina.

"Hey," Christopher said in a dismissive tone. He didn't even glance in her direction. That made Sabrina swoon even harder. She swore he never looked sexier than at that moment, smiling down at her with the light of the bonfire flickering in his eyes.

Gina must have sensed she wasn't wanted there and started in on Sabrina, noticing something about her was slightly off. "Is that our head cheerleader *drunk* already?"

"Lay off it, Gina," Christopher said, swiveling his head to blast her with a cold stare.

She relished it, smiling at the fact that she'd finally captured his attention, even if it was negative.

"Yeah," Sabrina butted in with a slight slur, "*shut up*, Gina."

Gina balked in her usual, overly dramatic way. "Shut up? I was just, like, looking out for the *integrity* of the team, that's all. We're supposed to be here to help raise the spirit of the school for, like, Homecoming and all that. I'm just surprised, I really am. I would have thought our leader would be here in, like, top form to, you know, *lead* and be a beacon for Thompson Point. Sorry for being concerned!"

"What are you on?" Christopher asked. "Look around you. Almost *everyone* has a beer in their hands. They are here to party. Right now, no one gives a *shit* about school spirit."

"*Oh*, Christopher," Gina said with a playful smirk. "Come on now, you *know* what I mean. Mister big, strong quarterback!"

"Why don't . . . why don't you just go away, Gina?" Sabrina stood up from the log, and the entire ground seemed to shift with her. Her arms shot out from her sides to help keep her balance. Gina laughed.

"What, are you gonna, like, make me? You can hardly stand."

"Gina," Christopher said sternly. He narrowed his eyes at her like a parent scolding a child. And just like a bratty little girl, Gina continued to try to play it off with her wide-eyed, 'Who me?' charade.

"I'm just saying," Gina replied, hands up in protest, "if *I* was head cheerleader, I wouldn't be bumbling around like that. I would, like, carry myself with poise and grace."

Something within Sabrina snapped. Maybe it was the alcohol, or Gina's stupid, smug look, or the way she was blatantly flirting with Christopher *and* lobbing insults, or a combination of all three, but before she was even cognizant of what she was doing, Sabrina was up in her face.

"Is that the same poise and grace you used when you *attacked* me in the school's basement bathroom!?"

"When I what!?" Gina asked, her toying innocence molding into pure confusion.

"You know what I'm talking about!" Sabrina yelled, waving an accusatory finger right under Gina's nose. "Or was it that easy for you to, like, forget? Where's my choker, by the way? What did you do with it?"

"Your *stupid, ugly,* necklace? Is that what you're going on about? What the hell would I want with that tasteless trash you tried to pass off as fashion? I wouldn't be caught *dead* in that thing."

"You cut it right off my neck with a knife!" Sabrina screamed with tears starting to form at the edges of her eyes. Her arms flailed wildly, seemingly of their own accord. Everything spun around her in a dizzying whirlwind, the light and shadows blurred together.

"*Whoa, whoa*, Sabrina, what are you talking about?" Christopher asked, his hands around her waist.

"Her!" She pointed at Gina, unable to stop the tears now rolling down her cheeks. "She did it!"

"It's time you went home and stopped embarrassing yourself," Gina taunted.

"I think it is time I got you out of here," Christopher said. "Come on."

"No," Sabrina said, violently shaking her head. "Not until I get it back."

"Get what back?" Christopher asked, slightly annoyed that his night was going every which way *except* the way he'd planned.

"My choker!" Sabrina cried. "The lioness!"

Gina chuckled. "I already told you, I don't have your stupid necklace. I don't know what it was that, like, *possessed* you to think I took it, but I didn't."

With gritted teeth and a surge of the lioness rushing through her, Sabrina wrenched herself from Christopher's grip and pumped her arm back, ready to send a fist straight across Gina's pompous, bratty little mouth. Christopher caught her hand before it could make contact, scooping Sabrina up and tossing her over his shoulder.

"That's enough! Time to go!"

"Cat fight!" someone yelled. By that point, a crowd had gathered around the girls, watching them feud with drunken, eager eyes. As Sabrina squirmed on his shoulder, Christopher forged an exit path, pushing through the shadowed barrier of his peers. With a unified groan, everyone dispersed, disappointed the fight had ended before any blood could be shed.

Gina stood rooted in place, a look of total shock frozen on her face. "Did she really just try to swing on me? Like, for real?"

Christopher carried Sabrina back to the car, stomping his way through the darkened trail by moonlight and instinct.

"I'm worried about you," he said, climbing into the driver's seat after carefully setting her down and buckling her in. "What was that all about?"

Sabrina leaned back against the headrest, her wet cheeks smeared with dripping black lines of eyeliner and smudged makeup. Christopher hadn't started the car yet, but it felt like they were moving. She closed her eyes, wishing everything would slow down and be still.

"Why did I say that?" she whispered. "Maybe it wasn't her."

"What?" Christopher asked. He stared out the windshield, the keys dangling from his right hand as he held the steering wheel.

"I don't know anymore," Sabrina said before slipping into a fit of uncontrollable sobbing. "It was a few weeks ago . . . I . . . I went to the basement bathroom at school because . . . because . . ."

Christopher wrapped his arms around her and pulled her close to him. He rubbed her back as her crying intensified. "It's okay," he consoled, "let it all out. Tell me what's going on."

Sabrina sniffled, trying to gather the space for words. There was so much to say. All of this had been building up inside, and now it was bubbling over, ready to spill through the cracks, splintering across her foundation.

She hadn't told *anyone* what had happened. But it was there, in Christopher's car, with his body and arms shielding her from the chilly night air that nibbled at the edges of the open top, that she knew he was safe to tell. He held her in silence, waiting until she could calm herself enough to speak.

Sabrina kept her head pressed into his chest. Then, fighting through her tears and bouts of heaves, she told him everything: the first suspected observation of a darkened shape moving about her bushes, the continued shadows dancing on her periphery, the hushed lullabies drifting through her window, the knot of unease that had tightened as summer burned itself onward, and finally, the incident in the bathroom, the way the intruder had barged in and dragged her out of the stall, of how scared and vulnerable she had felt as the knife was dragged across her neck, how playfully the blade had moved, toying and taunting her before sliding underneath her choker and . . .

"*Oh*, Sabrina, I'm so sorry about all this. But *why* didn't you tell me about it?" Christopher tightened his embrace.

"I . . . I . . ." It was nearly impossible for her to say anything more. Not right now. Her entire body shook, not the dizzy spells from the beer, but full-on tremors from her nervous system going haywire.

"Tomorrow," Christopher said. "We *have* to tell

someone about it tomorrow. The police. If there's some kind of psycho out there, they need to know. You have to file a report. I'll go with you."

Sabrina didn't answer. She wanted to remain in the warmth of his body. Christopher shifted slightly and put the keys in the ignition. With her head now leaning on his shoulder, he backed out of the spot and began the drive back to her house.

At some point, as the car cruised through the dark and quiet streets, Sabrina passed out.

Chapter 12

Where was Christopher?

Sabrina had slept through most of yesterday. When she'd finally awoken, her head was pounding, and her throat was as dry as sandpaper. She'd trudged to the bathroom, where she filled a glass of water from the sink and chugged it down in seconds.

Pieces of the night before drifted around in her brain like loose sediment in a lake. She recalled the bonfire, though now it felt like some fuzzy, faraway dream, like a sensation of a memory that had been manufactured. There was the scuffle with Gina, though what she had *actually* said was completely lost on her. And then Christopher had brought her home and . . .

She had told him everything.

He was supposed to come over and help her; that much she did remember. She'd called his house, and his mom had answered in that sweet, mousey voice of hers, but said she hadn't seen him all day. She figured he was out with friends somewhere.

Sabrina didn't think too much of it, and besides, she felt like a truck had slammed into her body and spent the rest of the afternoon and evening in bed, watching some TV and relaxing.

But that was yesterday. Now it was Monday, and he *still* hadn't even given her a courtesy call to see how she was doing. That wasn't like him. He hadn't been waiting for her by their lockers either, which was their usual morning meeting spot before school began.

Maybe he's just a bit late today?

Sabrina knew he wasn't skipping school. If there had been some sort of plan, he would have *definitely* reached out and begged her to join him. She wouldn't, of course, but she would let him try to persuade her. Even with her new look, her *alteration*, there were some things, core tenets, that could not be changed. She had *never* skipped school, and with all she had going on and everything she had built up and strived for, she didn't plan to start now, even if it *was* her senior year.

Sabrina gasped when she strolled into Ms. Pike's class. First, there was Gina, perched in her front row seat, her nose turned up, lips curved into a nasty scowl, with her eyes spitting hateful flames. Sabrina moved quickly to her desk, averting any further glances at Gina, only to realize the seat behind hers was empty. *Christopher's seat.*

It was nearly 11 AM at that point. Even Christopher had never been that late to school. So where was he then?

"Good morning, class!" Ms. Pike greeted, practically singing. She held up the baby doll, and its eyes rolled open. "Today is the day! *Someone* is going to be a parent! I have already pulled names from a hat and assembled the order of the students. But before we get to the lucky person that gets to start this project, I want to go over a few things about this baby doll."

A collective groan sounded through the classroom. Ms. Pike ignored it. Sabrina couldn't help but notice how bubbly she was, prancing around the front of her desk with the doll in her arms. The way her face beamed, the smile spread across, the twinkle in her eye, something was up.

Did she get a new boyfriend or something? Sabrina wondered.

"First thing, because I *know* someone is going to try," Ms. Pike started, "there is no on and off button on this doll. Once it is activated, which I've already done, it is on. You can't switch the baby off and think you're going to skate on by. And don't even *think* about trying to remove the batteries. If you do, I will know."

"But, like, how could you possibly know if someone took the batteries out or not?" Billy asked with a snicker, apparently having learned nothing from Ms. Pike's prior outburst.

"Don't worry about how *I* will know. Worry about the fact that if you do, not only would you fail but . . ." Ms. Pike's neck twisted, and her head bent sideways for a moment. "You'd have a lot of other problems to deal with as well. *Don't do it.*"

Billy opted to keep quiet and leaned back in his chair.

Sabrina kept glancing at the door, hoping Christopher might stroll in with a late pass. What if Ms. Pike picked him first to take the baby? Would *she* have to bring it to him since he wasn't there?

Ms. Pike laid the baby doll down on her desk for a moment, plucking a light blue bag from somewhere off the floor and setting it down next to the battery-operated infant. Opening it up, she began to pull various accessories from inside, arranging them across the top of her desk like she was setting up some roadside attraction selling baby-themed trinkets. Keeping her eyes focused on Ms. Pike's spread of items so as not to catch another scorch from Gina's flamethrowing death stare, Sabrina watched her pick up a bottle first.

"Your bag will come with three specially designed bottles. They are to be filled with water *only*. If you fill it with something else, thinking you're going to be funny, you're going to be sorry. There is a sensor that will detect that it is not water and immediately reject it. Yes, that means the doll will vomit whatever it is you tried to feed it."

A sensor that can tell if it's water or not? This thing really is high-tech! There's no way something like this was cheap. How was the school able to afford it? Was it that important that we learned the value of raising a baby during high school? And where the heck is Christopher? Why isn't he here!?

"The baby will need to eat three times a day. All you need to do is bring the nipple of the bottle to its lips and tip it like this." Ms. Pike demonstrated, scooping the baby doll into her arms and pushing the bottle to its mouth. In response, it started suckling, draining the water within. Once again, Sabrina was amazed at its realness. The way its little fingers gripped the sides of the bottle and how those tiny, baby lips cupped around the nipple, chugging the liquid. Once the bottle was empty, Ms. Pike gently pulled it away and set it on her desk.

"After each feeding, you will need to burp the baby." Ms. Pike performed this next step, holding the baby doll near her shoulder and patting its back. A couple of the boys in class giggled when the doll released a low belch. Continuing to pat its back, she let them have their laugh. It let out a few more burps before Ms. Pike returned it to the top of her desk.

It cooed and kicked its legs before it launched into a full-on crying fit. Sabrina watched as most of the kids in class pressed their hands over their ears. The shrieking sound was irritating, but what truly caught her off guard were the wet lines dribbling out of the doll's eyes.

The doll cries actual *tears?*

Sabrina was stunned. She couldn't believe all the things the doll could do. All the bells and whistles it came with. Real tears? Was that why it drank bottles of water? To reroute internally and use it as tears?

"Now it's time to change the baby," Ms. Pike announced, hovering over the thrashing baby doll as it continued to cry like a banshee. She undid the sides of its diaper and opened it up.

Billy's hand shot straight up. "*Um*, by the way, is it a girl or a boy?"

"Neither," Ms. Pike said as she picked up the now naked baby doll and showed it off to the class. "You can decide when it's your turn."

It had no defining genitalia and instead had a small hole in the skin between its legs where Sabrina assumed more water must come out to imitate pee. As Ms. Pike continued to explain, she learned she was correct in that assumption. The diapers were reusable cloth ones that would eventually dry up.

Once the baby was in a fresh diaper, Ms. Pike plucked a pacifier from the accessory display and placed it in the baby doll's mouth. Just like the bottle nipple, the lips started suckling, the pacifier bobbing up and down.

Ms. Pike gently rocked the baby doll as she paced between the rows of students, and eventually it closed its eyes and fell asleep. She kept it there, nestled into the crook of her arm, the pacifier's rapid movements slowing as its lips relaxed and its arms went limp.

"And now we let this little cherub sleep until it gets hungry again," Ms. Pike said softly. "But by the time the next feeding comes, it will be one of *your* responsibilities."

Eyes bounced all over the classroom. Everyone was wondering who was going to be called first. Beneath her desk, Sabrina crossed her fingers. Caring for the baby doll was one of the *last* things she wanted right now.

Homecoming was fast approaching, and there was just too much going on. Too much to do! Between banners and signs that still needed to be painted and hung, the pep rally spirit cheer still needed sprucing up, not to mention the *other* cheering routines for the big football game and the final details for the dance. None of it was going to be easy, especially now that things between her and Gina were even worse.

Maybe she'll pick Gina! she thought hopefully, her fingers still crossed. *That would be perfect! Then she'd have to sit out for Homecoming, and I could lead the team and the committee without any pushback or hassle.* A smirk crept across Sabrina's face as she pictured Gina feeding and burping the baby doll. She could imagine her disgusted face at having to change the thing and the wrinkles that would form under the eyes from long nights of endless shrieks and cries.

"And the lucky first student is . . ."

Everyone straightened up and leaned forward, hoping it would be anyone but themselves. Sabrina paused with bated breath.

Please pick Gina. Please pick Gina.

Thoughts of Gina struggling with the battery-powered baby doll continued to form in her head, distracting her from Ms. Pike's announcement. It wasn't until moments later, with the weight of all the eyes in the room upon her, that the realization hit.

"Congratulations!" Ms. Pike grinned immeasurably as she towered above Sabrina's desk, baby doll and bag in her arms, ready to hand them over.

She looked over at Gina, whose smile matched the width of their teacher's. The scorn in her face was gone, her eyes instead beaming with the triumph of victory. "Looks like *I'll* have to, like, step in as head cheerleader while *you* play mommy for a couple weeks," she snickered.

Sabrina groaned as Ms. Pike lowered the doll into her arms.

"Careful now, don't want to wake the baby prematurely," her teacher advised with a wink. She was all teeth at this point, her lips pulled back in a crescent shape.

Sabrina looked down at the sleeping baby doll, at

its soft, shut eyelids and perfectly curled lashes. Its chest gently pulsed in a steady rhythm.

Is it... breathing?

She didn't have time to observe or question any further. The bell sounded, and everyone stood to grab their books and backpacks, ready for their next class and glad that *they* weren't the ones tied down with a baby. They would get their turn, but not today.

Sabrina rose, cradling the doll in one arm as she swung her backpack over her shoulder and then grabbed the bag with all the baby supplies. As she made her way to the door, taking caution to not bump or disturb the baby's slumber, Ms. Pike watched on and waved by opening and closing her fingers against her thumb like a snapping mouth.

"I'm always here if you need anything," she offered, her fingered jaws slowing as if chewing on a hearty piece of meat. "Anything at all."

Sabrina didn't answer but nodded, hoping the bob of her head would be a satisfactory response. The baby doll shifted in her hold, and she gasped in surprise, but then it settled, nestling back to its restful state.

Could they make this thing any more real!? It moves in its sleep? And it breathes? Does it get into mischief too? Am I going to have to baby-proof my house for the next few weeks? Why did I have to be picked first?

"You'll be a great mom."

Sabrina stopped on the threshold, one step away from being in the hallway.

"What?"

"*You*," Ms. Pike answered. "You'll be a great mom, I can tell."

"*Oh,*" Sabrina said, completely weirded out. "Thank you?"

She took a final glimpse at her teacher and nodded again, taking note of Christopher's vacant seat before slipping away into the hallway.

Where are you when I need you most, Christopher?

Chapter 13

Rachel stared, eyes as wide as a deer frozen in the glare of oncoming headlights, as Sabrina plopped down across from her in the cafeteria, arms bundled with a baby.

"No way!" she shrieked in a high shrill, then, noticing the defeat in her friend's face, changed her tone. "I mean, *ugh*, *you* got picked to have the baby first? That *sucks*."

"I'm well aware," Sabrina replied, using her free hand to turn the accessory bag over in hopes it would suffice as a makeshift crib. She placed the sleeping baby doll on it, thankful for the momentary break.

"Was it random, or was there a reason she chose you first? Like, did she pick you because you're the best student in the school?" Rachel asked, genuinely curious.

"I don't know. Ms. Pike claims she pulled names at random and put a list together. I just . . ." Sabrina paused, rubbing the bridge of her nose. "Why did she have to choose *me*? I'm going to miss all of the homecoming festivities now, thanks to this!"

"I guess you were just the lucky name pulled first, then?"

"Yeah," Sabrina scoffed. "I've never won a contest in my life, but *now* my luck decides to just kick in? Wonderful."

"It's only for a few weeks, though, right? I can help you. And Christopher, too."

"He doesn't even know I have this thing. I haven't seen him since Saturday. He wasn't in class today. You haven't run into him, have you?"

"Me? No. Haven't seen him today. But we also don't have any classes together either."

Sabrina was about to answer when the doll stirred, opening its eyes and releasing a massive wail that shot through the cafeteria like a shockwave. She scooped up the crying doll in a frenzy, eager to escape the stares of the other students and stop the noise.

"Let me help you," Rachel said, but before she could lend a hand, Sabrina had piled everything in her arms and raced out the doors.

Cheeks flushed with embarrassment as she juggled the bawling thing and bag. She turned her head frantically in search of a quiet place to feed.

It had been a total of maybe one hour, and already she was over it. How was she supposed to enjoy *any* of the next few weeks with a whining, crying, hungry baby attached to her? She rushed into a desolate section of the south wing, tossing down the bag before sitting against a row of lockers. She unzipped it and felt around for a bottle, pulling one out that was thankfully already filled with water. The incessant crying rang out in her ears and bounced around the empty hallway like a scream swirling in a hollow cave.

She shoved the nipple into the baby doll's lips, and

it quieted immediately, sucking down the water in rapid gulps. While the baby ate, Sabrina tilted her head back against the locker, while Gina's devilish grin played in her mind over and over. She felt her grip on the bottle tighten.

Now it was Gina who was going to get all the glory. *She* was going to get to lead the team. *She* was going to get final say on the cheer for the pep rally. *She* was going to completely take over the committee planning. All thanks to this stupid, plastic thing.

Why me? Why me first? Doesn't Ms. Pike know how much I have going on? That I'm the head cheerleader? That I'm on the Homecoming committee? That it's my senior year and this is the last Homecoming I'll ever have? Is this project really more important than the memories I'll never be able to get back?

The option was always there. She *could* just fail. She could simply stop feeding the fake needy infant and let it "die". Except, of course, she couldn't. Failure wasn't a part of Sabrina's vocabulary. She'd never settled for anything less than a B+ in her entire life. No, she was going to see this through, even if it meant kicking and screaming and possibly crying herself the entire way. She knew that, and as the baby doll finished the last few drops of water in the bottle, she couldn't help but feel a small surge of hatred for it.

She wondered if all moms went through something similar. If when they looked at their babies, instead of feeling love and warmth, they felt disgust, seeing nothing more than some wretched parasite sucking away all their time and energy. Was there supposed to be an instant connection? Or did a mother's love take time to develop, like a Polaroid picture, blank and bare until slowly, it took shape and a clear, whole image appeared?

Sabrina wasn't sure. She wasn't a mother, and this wasn't a real baby. It might have *looked* and *felt* real, but in reality, it was just a doll. A sophisticated doll with a seemingly endless array of features, but a doll nonetheless. How was she supposed to love a complicated toy?

The rest of the day crawled by, not like a swift baby testing its newfound mobility, but in the pace of a stubborn tortoise. Luckily, after the lunchtime feeding, the baby doll had fallen back asleep and remained that way for all her afternoon classes. Still, she could hardly concentrate on anything her teachers said.

Her brain was focused on getting out of there. Of getting home, flopping onto her bed, and pulling the phone off her side table to call Christopher. She wanted to hear his voice. To hear his answer for not calling her yesterday.

They still had to go down to the police station and file a report. She didn't want to go without him. Being the star quarterback carried a weight with it, not that Sabrina's achievements were lacking in any regard, but she knew the people in Thompson Point paid more attention to the football team. Cheerleaders were cute and all, but people *respected* the players. With Christopher there beside her, she felt like the police might take her report a little more seriously, *especially* since she'd have a plastic tot in tow now.

The final bell was a welcome blessing. She gathered her things and bolted toward the student parking lot, not bothering to catch up with Rachel in the halls like she normally would *or* supervise the cheering practice. Maybe tomorrow, once she had figured out some sort of routine, but another feeding was due soon, and the last thing she wanted was a screaming baby interrupting her team. Gina could lead things today, as much as it pained Sabrina to let her do so.

As she made her way across the lot to her car, she couldn't help but notice the darkening clouds gathering above. She quickened her pace, racing to beat the impending rain. If it was luck that had put her name at the top of Ms. Pike's list, then she was now fresh out. The clouds let loose with a torrential downpour mere seconds before she reached her car door.

She fumbled with her keys, trying to finagle them out of her jeans pocket as she balanced the baby and bag in her arms through the pelting rain. Once unlocked, she slid her backpack from her shoulders and whipped it into the backseat. Then, with her mind absolutely frazzled, she tossed the accessory bag *and* the baby doll onto the passenger seat.

Glancing in the rearview mirror, she noticed her makeup running down her face, and her hair was a sopping mess, like she was fresh out of a shower. She shivered, her clothes dripping and sticking to her skin. It wasn't until she had pulled out of the parking lot and her car was winding down the hill toward the main road that she heard the baby start to whimper and realized she had thrown the doll on the seat with the same complacency as a sack of groceries.

Why now? Sabrina thought, pushing the car a few miles over the speed limit despite the onslaught of rain. Her car sped along the slick, wet streets, spraying waves of water into the air as the tires sliced through deep puddles. Now the doll was screeching. If it had an actual throat, by now it would be hoarse and raw. But instead, much to her dismay, it could seemingly cry forever. Or at least as long as the batteries lasted.

Sabrina shuddered, trying to imagine the torture of listening to a baby weep and howl for years on end. From what she'd experienced already, a few weeks were enough to drive her insane.

"Just a minute, please! Hold on, baby, almost there." She had to laugh. The whole thing was just absurd.

Look at me, talking to this thing like it's a real baby!

She turned onto her street and pulled into the driveway. Once parked, she dashed across the lawn, using the bag to shield the baby doll from the rain.

To her surprise, the front door opened, and Sabrina hurried up the porch steps and into the house to find her mom there in the entryway, as though she'd been awaiting her arrival.

"*Oh!*" her mom gasped. "There's a screaming baby!"

"Yeah, it's that health project I told you about. Guess who got picked first." She rolled her eyes, half expecting her mom to spout off some phrase about crying babies that she'd been keeping tucked away for the proper occasion.

"Well, listen," her mom said somberly. "Not to change gears so suddenly, but there's something I need to tell you. It's about Christopher."

Sabrina froze in her tracks, her breath caught in her throat.

Christopher?

"What about him?"

"He's... *Oh* gosh, I don't know how to say this, Sabrina. Right now, he's at Thompson Point Memorial Hospital in a coma. His mother called here a few minutes ago. They... they found his car last night, smashed into a tree around the bend at Hallows Road."

I was so close to you that night at the bonfire. I wanted to reach out and run my fingers through your hair. I wanted to caress your soft, perfect skin as it warmed by the fire. The beer on your breath was so potent. Mixed together with the cherry-scented gloss spread across your lips, you were like a whole new flavor. I wanted to try it. If the risk of being caught and ruining the entire plan wasn't there, I would've licked my tongue along your mouth, just to see how you taste. Maybe it would give me an insight into your perfection.

It's amazing how clueless people can be when the drinks are flowing and the darkness of night takes command. I walked among you in the shadows, and you had no idea. No one did. All it takes is a simple wig, a different outfit, and some makeup, and it's like I'm one of you all. I could be anyone.

I watched as that little wench, Gina, approached and started a fight. I might have to do something about her, too. Can't have someone harming my perfect little vessel now, can we? She was out of line. Another that can't match up to you, Sabrina.

I followed as Christopher brought you home and carried your sleeping body into the house. That was when I slipped into his backseat and waited, lying low and out of sight.

Then he returned, and I let him drive for a bit. I waited until we were surrounded by trees. Then I sprang up and covered his eyes. He screamed, and the car swerved all over the road. I wasn't worried. I knew I would be protected. That was part of the promise.

I didn't let go until it was too late. The last thing Christopher saw was the giant tree before the car smashed into it. I watched the windshield splinter as he folded over the steering wheel and his head impacted the glass. Blood was pouring down the sides of his face. It was glorious. I couldn't let it go to waste.

Before any more precious seconds could tick by, I reached into the crossbody satchel I'd brought along to retrieve an empty vial. I unscrewed the cap and pressed it to his cheek, collecting the stream of blood until it was filled. Then I disappeared into the night, leaving him to bleed out. My task was done. I'd gotten what I needed.

What did you see in him, Sabrina? He was never good enough for you. Surely you knew that, didn't you? You can't convince me the thought didn't linger somewhere in your mind. But that's okay, he's been taken care of. Someone will find his car soon enough. The word will get out.

The next phase is in motion. One down, two to go.

The blood of three. That was part of its demands. Part of what is required to complete the ritual. What I must offer to that smile in the darkness. To the teeth in the night.

A personal object . . .

A sample of skin or hair . . .

The blood of three . . .

And finally, flesh of the asker . . .

Me. My flesh. I would happily give any body part for what I am promised.

I'm so close . . .

Christopher was so easy to dispose of. The crash, the shattered glass, and the blood—it excited me. I anticipate the next vial will be even easier to fill. The blood brings me one step closer. And then I can get what is owed to me.

Sabrina, my prize lies within you.

Chapter 14

Sabrina fed and changed the baby doll on the ride over to the hospital. Everything felt so disconnected, free-floating and unreal. Her hands seemed to move independently from her brain as she performed the diaper change in her lap, switching the damp cloth for a new, clean one without even looking. Instead, her eyes stared vacantly ahead, seeing but not comprehending the streets and sidewalks obscured by the sheets of rain smattering the windshield.

Physically, Sabrina was in the car, but her mind was elsewhere. Up and away in the black clouds, soaking in the storm outside. Thoughts piled up in her head like a massive car crash, each piece of twisted metal a new fear or worry.

As her mom pulled the car into the parking lot and the hospital loomed ahead, it was like her brain had been slingshotted back into her body. She felt the weight of its impact and pressed at her temples as it jostled around inside her skull. The baby doll was quiet, seemingly satisfied, but not asleep. Its eyes watched her, whether she was aware or not. It blinked and breathed.

The car stopped next to the hospital's main

entrance. Sabrina hesitated with her hand on the door handle. Reality surrounded the car like a rabid dog foaming at the mouth. She didn't want to get out. If she did, she was going to get bitten.

"Go on, honey," her mom coaxed gently.

The baby kicked its legs in her lap. Gulping a giant breath of air, Sabrina propped the baby up against one of her shoulders and opened the door. Once outside the vehicle, she bent down to grab the accessory bag from the floor. It was docile for now, but who knew how long that would last? All she needed was a tantrum in the hospital to truly send her over the edge.

"Get in there and see him. Even . . . even in a coma . . . he'll feel your presence. Just you being there will help him. Love is the most healing energy of all. I'll park the car and come find you." Her mom reached across the passenger seat and closed the door from the inside. Then she drove off in search of a parking spot. Clutching the baby doll in one hand and carrying the accessory bag in the other, Sabrina trudged toward the entrance. An awning above the walkway held off the rain, so at least she could make it inside without getting soaked, though she was in such a daze it likely wouldn't have phased her anyway.

The last thing she expected to see as the glass doors slid open was Lawrence, donning a *Thompson Point House of Pizza* uniform, exiting the building. He seemed equally surprised to see her, especially with the plastic bundle of joy cradled against her shoulder.

He stopped suddenly, as if hitting an invisible wall. "Hi . . . Sabrina."

"What are you doing here, Lawrence? Were you here to see Christopher?" She didn't necessarily mean for it to come across as rude, but she also didn't apologize for her tone either. The fact that he was wearing a pizza delivery uniform didn't fully click in her brain. Her focus was on Christopher. She needed to find him. To see him. Lawrence was like a pothole in the road she hadn't noticed until it was too late. The hospital doors started to close but were forced open at the halfway point as a woman in scrubs hurried out, likely a nurse whose shift had just ended.

"Christopher? Like your boyfriend? No. I, uh..." Lawrence pointed at the logo stitched onto the breast pocket of his shirt of a slice of pizza oozing with gooey, dripping cheese. "I was delivering a pizza to one of the doctors."

"*Oh*," Sabrina said with a nod.

Of course, he wasn't here to see Christopher, she thought, mentally smacking her head for saying that out loud. *They aren't friends. Why else would he be here except to deliver a pizza?*

Lawrence shuffled his feet, wracking his brain for something else to say. Beads of sweat built up on his forehead despite the late September chill ushering in the early autumn season. He removed his hat that had the same pizza logo and combed his fingers through his greasy hair.

"Well..." He started to say something, but another voice interrupted him.

"Sabrina! You're still out here? I thought you'd already be in there by now. Come on, let's go find his room." It was her mom.

"I have to go," Sabrina said, this time much softer.

"Right," Lawrence said. He tipped his hat at her before jetting off toward his car in the pounding rain.

Sabrina's mom pulled up beside her, placing a hand on her shoulder, and together they walked into the hospital to find out where Christopher was.

They checked in at the reception desk and, after a few minutes, were guided by one of the nurses to his room. The closer they got, the more Sabrina's stomach tightened. That dog of reality, that vicious hound of certain misfortune, was right on her heels now, licking its teeth and snapping its jaws. She could hear its deep, throaty growl intermingled with the *beeps* and *boops* of the hospital machinery. There was no escaping it now. It was only a matter of steps until they'd be in Christopher's room. She would *see* him in the hospital bed, and then the dog would chomp down on her ankles, and there would be no way to stop the bleeding.

The nurse left them at the door, and Sabrina's mom quietly knocked before they entered. Christopher's entire family surrounded his hospital bed, blocking the view of his body. They all turned their heads as the door swung open.

"*Oh*, Sabrina," his mom greeted through tears, stepping forward to hug her. She placed the baby doll onto the counter that ran alongside the wall next to the door, dropped the accessory bag, and accepted the embrace, squeezing tightly as though she were hugging Christopher himself. "Thank you for coming."

"I'm so sorry, Brenda. What . . . what happened?" Sabrina managed, her voice muffled by his mom's shoulder.

"The police... They found his car wrapped around a tree off Hallows Road. And now..." They parted but remained close. "And now my baby boy is..."

Brenda's face was like a shattered mirror, and it nearly broke Sabrina. Ever since they'd met the first time Christopher had invited her over for dinner, Sabrina had always thought his mom was beautiful. She was a former pageant queen and continued to carry herself in that same fashion: her copper hair always done, makeup always on, and a strut that was the textbook definition of confidence. Now, all that was out the window. Sabrina could feel her fragility as though she were nothing more than rattling pieces of broken porcelain beneath her clothes. There was no question about her love for Christopher. Sabrina had no doubt in her mind that when he was born, the connection his mom felt was instant.

Christopher's dad came over to offer a hug as well. He wasn't crying at the moment, but she could tell he had been prior. His normally rugged face was softened, and he trembled when he wrapped his arm around her.

Christopher's sister, Candice, remained by his bedside. She was a freshman, and whenever Sabrina saw her in the halls, they would wave to one another. She knew Candice was into volleyball and learning how to play guitar, but those were facts she had pulled from small talk at the dinner table. She really didn't know her much at all, but Sabrina reached over and rubbed her shoulder, and Candice nodded with tears welling in her eyes. No matter how well they knew one another, they were connected now, bonded by the tragedy of Christopher's accident.

And then Sabrina inched closer and finally saw him. Christopher was motionless on the bed with his gorgeous hair hidden behind a covering of bandages over the top of his head. One side of his face was bruised in a deep shade of purple like a bad piece of fruit in the produce aisle. But it was the breathing tube shoved down his throat that really made Sabrina lose it. She collapsed to the ground, sobbing uncontrollably as waves of guilt crashed over her.

This is all my fault! He was taking care of me because I had had a few drinks, and he must have been so exhausted driving home. Did he fall asleep behind the wheel? Is that what happened? Oh, Christopher, if only I could've known. I would have never gotten so messy. I just wanted to forget. What if... Sabrina didn't want to imagine it, but the thought crawled in regardless, expanding like a balloon until it pressed against the sides of her skull. *What if he never wakes up? What if that... that tube is the only thing keeping his body going? I'd never be able to live with myself.*

Sabrina's mom rushed over to help her up and sat her down in the empty chair beside Christopher's bed.

Sabrina held onto the guardrail as she cried. Everyone in the room was crying now.

She thought about what her mom had said on the ride over to the hospital. About how he would be able to feel her presence.

Love is the most healing energy of all.

Did she love Christopher? She'd never said "I love you" to him. At this point, they'd only been dating for four months. But seeing him lying there, still as a statue, she realized she *did* love him. Maybe she wasn't *in* love, not yet, but something was there. Was it enough? Could he feel her heartbeat radiate like ghostly waves? Could she *actually* heal him?

She wanted to believe she could. Lately, all she wanted to do was flee from her parents' phrases and advice, but this one? This was something she wanted to be true. She was going to hold onto this.

Across the room, on the counter, the baby doll cooed. Sabrina glanced up, but her vision was distorted, like staring through a waterfall. She brushed the tears away and looked again. Things were still a tad hazy but clearer. She could see the doll resting on the counter. It had turned its head to the side and was gazing at Sabrina, almost as if to say, *"Hey, you forgot me over here. I'm just a baby, remember?"*

But wait, was it . . . smiling?

It emitted a squeaky baby laugh from its wide spread pink lips. No one else seemed to notice or paid any attention. The heavy sadness swelling the room tethered them to Christopher. Their focus was solely on him.

It squealed again and reached up to grab its wiggling toes. Its face beamed, lips held open in a toothless, gummy grin, its pudgy cheeks puffed out with pink flesh. Why was it doing that? She knew it could suckle a bottle and that it would cry and make noises, but she didn't recall Ms. Pike having mentioned anything about open-mouthed expressions or grabbing its toes.

I'm not imagining it, right? There's something strange going on with that baby. Why is it smiling?

Sabrina straightened in the chair, leaning forward to inspect the doll as best as she could from where she sat. That was when she noticed its eyes. She gasped, but it went unnoticed, swallowed by the vacuum of sadness in the room. Its pupils were angled upward, not looking at her but *beyond* her, next to her.

They were fixated on Christopher.

Chapter 15

Sabrina didn't go to school the next day. Under normal circumstances, tarnishing her perfect attendance record, especially during her senior year when the finish line was in sight, was unfathomable. Simply out of the question. A possibility never even considered. The girl she'd been her entire life and in many ways still was, wouldn't dream of ruining such a flawless streak. But the circumstances were far from normal, and her spirits were so dampened that even if she were to receive the Nobel Peace Prize today, she would've skipped out on accepting it.

After not seeing her face in the kitchen that morning before heading off to work, her mom and dad popped in to check on her, and when she told them she needed a day to rest, they nodded and understood.

"A day in bed to soothe the head," her dad said, smiling as he leaned down and planted a kiss in the tangles of her hair.

"We love you, Sabrina. I'll call and check on you shortly, okay? I know your mind is busy worrying about Christopher, and that's a lot for you. We can visit him again tomorrow if you want. I know he would like that. Rest up." Her mom felt her forehead, just to make sure it wasn't overly warm, which thankfully it wasn't. She kissed her cheek, and then together they quietly shut her door.

Sabrina sank her head into her pillow and shut her eyes. The doll lay beside her, resting after a much too early 4 A.M. feeding and changing. She hoped the doll might be able to sense how exhausted she was, both mentally and physically, and just . . . leave her alone for today.

That was impossible, of course, and she knew that. Even with all its bells and whistles and laundry list of features, there was no way it could *sense* what she was feeling. Just like a real baby, it was only concerned with its own needs. It only reacted out of hunger, or a wet diaper, or the necessity of a nap.

Still, she figured it couldn't hurt to put that ripple of a thought out into the universe. Maybe it would work the same way her mom said that Christopher would feel her presence in the hospital. Maybe it was something she could manifest.

Either way, what she really wanted now was to fall back asleep while the baby was being quiet before it was too late. The only problem was her head wouldn't stop swirling with thoughts and emotions. There was no stopping the guilt that flooded her. She kept analyzing the situation from every angle, but no matter which way she dissected it, each outcome was the same: *it was her fault*. Too many *if-only* scenarios played out in her mind, each a new possibility where maybe, just maybe, Christopher wasn't in a coma and was instead smiling at her from behind his football helmet as he prepared for the big homecoming game.

If only I had kept my cool and not lashed out at Gina.

If only I hadn't drunk those beers.

If only I hadn't had to pee, I never would have gone down to the basement, and I wouldn't have been attacked...

If only...

The phone rang on the bedside table beside her. Sabrina flailed in a panic, swooping the phone from its cradle in fear that the ringing might wake the doll.

"Hey, Mom," she greeted with assumption as she put the receiver to her ear.

"Mom? Sabrina, it's Rachel. I was calling to see how you were doing. You aren't at school, and everyone is talking about Christopher's accident, and I just wanted to make sure you were okay." Rachel's voice whispered through the phone in breathy bursts. "Sorry if I'm too quiet. I'm in the school office. I told Mrs. Steiner that I needed to call my parents."

"I appreciate you checking on me," Sabrina returned in the same volume of voice, eyeing the baby doll resting next to her. A warmth passed through her body from Rachel's gesture. "But I'm definitely not okay. I went to see him at the hospital yesterday, and *oh*, Rachel, it was so awful! He's just lying there covered in bandages with a breathing tube in his mouth. They don't know if he'll wake up or not."

Tears threatened to escape her eyes, but she pushed them back. At this point, she wasn't even sure how her body was able to conjure more up. She felt drained and dried out.

"I'm so sorry, Sabrina," Rachel said. "I really can't

imagine how you must feel. The whole school is sad today. But I'm here for you in any way I can be."

"Thank you," Sabrina said with a sniffle. The fight didn't last too long. Now the wet lines trailed from her eyes and rolled down her cheeks.

"I'll tell you one thing, Gina is turning into a real *monster*. I might have to quit the homecoming committee."

"I didn't think she could get any worse."

"You'd be surprised. Between you getting stuck with the baby and now Christopher... well, you already know..." Rachel let out a heavy sigh that came through as a distorted crackle on Sabrina's end. "If her head grows any bigger, she might just float off into the sky."

"She'd be doing us all a favor."

"You're right. Maybe she *will* be her own undoing. Anyway, I gotta go. Mrs. Steiner is staring at me from the front desk. I hope you'll be in school tomorrow, but don't push it. Either way, want to have a girls' night on Friday? My parents are going out. Why don't you come over? We could order a pizza, do our nails, and maybe rent a couple of videotapes? *Ooh!* How about something with Brad Pitt or Tom Cruise, or a cheesy romance flick? What do you say?"

It sounded like the type of distraction Sabrina could use right now. But how was she supposed to try and enjoy herself with the baby doll there? She was about to protest when Rachel spoke up again, as though they were telepathically linked through the telephone wires.

"*I* will help you take care of the baby doll. Don't

you worry about a thing. Girls' night. Friday. Okay? Gotta go, love ya!"

The phone call ended with a *click*, and Sabrina placed the phone back in its cradle. She dried her damp cheeks with the back of her arm and then closed her eyes. Her muscles eased up, and her body loosened and seemed to sink into the mattress.

Maybe my mom was right, Sabrina thought lucidly as she teetered on the edge of sleep. *Maybe love is the most healing energy.* She had certainly felt Rachel's love and care, like soft hands reaching through the telephone. It was enough to temporarily keep all the stress and sadness at bay, at least for a little while. A sleepover with her best friend sounded like the best medicine.

Without realizing it, Sabrina dozed off, so deeply and soundly she might as well have been dead. It was what her body needed. A hibernation from the world. Completely shut off.

She was pulled so deep into the dreamworld that she never noticed the baby doll start to roll back and forth beside her. Never felt the kick of its little feet. Never heard its first round of cries, like sirens calling out for its mother. It continued to screech, piercing the silence of the room with a painful, searing wail. Sabrina's body didn't even flinch.

It screamed and screamed, ramping up in intensity as if it were on fire. It screamed until *someone* stepped forth from the darkness and soothed it with a bottle.

Ah, so this is what it's like inside your house. So comfy, so cozy, so ... homely. You were raised with love, Sabrina. I already knew you came from a place of light. I'd already felt and seen your radiance, but this house ... no, this home *confirms it.*

I see a recent family portrait on the wall and dozens of other framed pictures of you over the years. I especially love this one ... it looks like you are at summer camp, maybe? You are jumping off a dock, arms and legs spread wide, you almost look like you are flying, and your smile is as wide as the sun is bright. Your smile has always been electric.

I knew you were the right choice.

As I make my way up the stairs to the second floor, I see another picture of you in your cheering uniform, posing with your pom poms. I know how much you like cheering. You're so good at it. I've seen the way you move. The way you command your team. It's your smile, once again, that draws me in. Your energy is magnetic. You look like you've never had to experience true pain before, and I'm sorry that that's all I have in store for you.

But it wasn't fair for me either. All the pain that I had to endure.

I can see it from the top of the stairs. It's your room,

Sabrina. All is quiet as I make my way down the hall and slowly open the door.

I have to stifle a gasp. I can't believe I'm in your room. There have been glimpses through the window, but it doesn't compare to actually being here on the other side of the glass. I have long dreamt of this. All those nights in the bushes, singing my songs, calling out to you. But now here I am, and there you are, sleeping like an angel with your precious cherub beside you.

Look at you, like a princess encased in crystal, like a queen kissed by the Sandman's dust, skin so soft, your hair spread out on the pillow like an auburn crown.

What do you dream of in that head of yours, my perfect vessel? Does my knife still dance in dreamlike lines across your neck, or is it now the pain of Christopher's eternal sleep that haunts your slumbering brainwaves? Do my lullabies sing in the landscapes of your mind? When you close your eyes, who's there smiling in the darkness? Is it me? Oh, I *hope so.*

I run a finger through your hair. How immaculate it is. I open up my satchel and pull out a container and a pair of scissors. Then, as delicately as I can, I cut a chunk of it. The sound of the scissors slicing through is satisfying. I place the strands in the container and put everything back in the satchel.

That's when the baby starts fussing. But you don't even move a muscle. Poor darling. Your body is overworked. Your nervous system is completely shot. Right now, you're as much in a coma as Christopher is. The baby cries for you. It screams bloody murder. But you, Sabrina, you remain blissfully unaware. You are locked in a dream.

I will allow you to sleep. Your body needs it. I need you in top shape. I pick the screaming infant up into my arms. As I slowly rock it back and forth, I scan your room for one of its bottles. At the foot of your bed, I see what looks to be a diaper bag. Inside, I find one of its bottles. I place the bottle nipple into the little rugrat's mouth, and it immediately quiets down, suckling away.

As the baby eats, I look around your room, at your lighted vanity mirror with your makeup accessories laid out, at your shelf of trophies, the posters on your walls of hunky celebrities, your neon-pink boombox alongside your stack of CDs, your bedside table with a telephone and alarm clock. This is your world, Sabrina. Thank you for sharing it with me. I feel privileged to get such an intimate look at your dwelling.

The baby is done with the bottle. It wriggles in my arms. Now I sing not to you, Sabrina, but to this child. To this beautiful baby of yours. You rest. My end of the bargain is almost complete. Thank you for your lovely hair. Two more vials of blood, and then the ritual can begin.

I'll offer it all up to the grinning teeth in the shadows. The smile in the darkness. And I will get what is owed to me. That's what it promised.

Oh, I have waited so long for this.

I'm ready for the pain to leave my body. For the agony to flee from my bones. For this nightmare to finally be over. To shed this happy mask and stop pretending. To feel a true bond.

I'm ready for you to give me what is mine. To deliver my beloved prize.

Sabrina, my vessel, my light, my savior, my everything.

The body and the blood, the flesh and the womb.

I kiss the baby on its forehead. Its eyelids flutter at my touch.

"Twinkle, twinkle little star . . .

How I wonder what you are . . .

Up above the world so high . . .
Like a diamond in the sky . . .
Twinkle, twinkle little star . . .
How I wonder what you are."

Chapter 16

Framed by the lights of her vanity mirror, Sabrina once again touched the bare spot on her neck where the lioness charm used to rest. It was not a reach made from habit, but this time with purpose. She was aware it was missing, painfully so, but needed, now more than ever, the strength of the formidable feline.

Her worst fear had been realized that morning as she sat before her reflection and began her daily ritual with her comb. She noticed on the third stroke, as the bristles sifted through her hair, that a particular section on her right side was shorter... *missing*. She dropped the comb and grabbed at her hair to inspect further, but there was no denying it. Her hair had been cut. *Someone* had taken a pair of scissors and cut off a chunk of it.

"No," she said with a gasp. "*Please*, no."

Pleading with her reflection didn't change anything. The horrifying reality sank into her stomach like a heavy stone in water.

The stalker is still out there. They were here... in my house... while I was sleeping...

The thought unnerved Sabrina to tears. She pulled

her hair back into a mock ponytail, clutching at the base of it with her fist. Unless someone was inspecting her head with the finesse of a seasoned homicide detective, no one would notice the violating trim with her hair like this. Satisfied, or as much as she could be through the tears and anxiety, she grabbed a black scrunchie off the counter of her vanity and plopped it in place.

The baby doll made a noise from atop her bed where she'd left it. It wasn't a cry, not yet anyway, but a short sound to make its presence known. It did that from time to time, much to Sabrina's annoyance, emitting nonsensical words and garbled sounds. She supposed real babies did that sort of thing too, but did the company that made this thing really need to nail *all* the details? Wasn't crying and feeding and rocking and having to change a doll enough? It really had to coo and thrash its arms and legs and laugh and smile?

Her thoughts shifted then to the hospital and the way the baby doll had seemed to stare at Christopher with those upturned lips, almost like it was relishing the fact that he was in a coma. But that was silly, right? It's a *doll*. Sabrina continually reminded herself of that fact. Sure, it was realistic—possibly a little too much—but at the end of the day, it was still just an overly-complicated toy that ran on batteries.

Still, it was the absolute last thing she needed with everything else going on. She'd already dried her eyes with a tissue and applied some eyeliner, but it was all for nothing because the tears gushed again, running curvy lines down her cheeks like flowing, black rivers.

None of it was fair. She was supposed to be leading the cheer team, and prepping for the homecoming festivities, and keeping Gina in her place, and canoodling with Christopher, and all the other *normal* things seventeen-year-old girls do during their senior year. All that was tainted now. Absolutely ruined.

She was really expected to care for this baby doll when her boyfriend was in a coma *and* she was being stalked by some mysterious person? Someone who had attacked her at school *and* been inside her house while she slept? Nowhere was safe. Where was she supposed to go?

"Sabrina, honey, how are you feeling this morning?" Her mom's voice asked after a soft knock on her door.

"I'm okay! I'll be right down," Sabrina answered, frantically grabbing some wet wipes to erase the makeup running down her face. She didn't want her parents to see her like this. What would she say? That someone broke into the house and cut her hair while she was asleep? That the same person had also attacked her in the bathroom? It really did sound crazy, even if she knew it was true. Still, *something* had to be done.

The only problem was the one person who knew anything was in a coma. Christopher couldn't help her anymore. Should she confide in Rachel? Sabrina had wanted to tell her, had *almost* told her so many times, but what held her back was bringing her best friend into the fold. What if, by telling her, it put the stalker's crosshairs on her, too?

Just then, a chilling realization bloomed in her head: *What if Christopher's accident wasn't an accident?*

The more she thought about it, the probability seemed likely. It was only *after* she had told Christopher everything and they had made plans to go to the police station together that he had his accident. *Had the stalker somehow heard Sabrina spill everything to him? Had they been listening somewhere in the shadows?*

The image of some unknown person hiding in the back of Christopher's car, drenched in darkness and eavesdropping on their every word, sent ice-cold shivers tingling down her spine.

So what was this then, some sort of retaliation? A way to keep her silent? Had she really put him in danger just by telling him about it? What had they done to his vehicle? How did they make Christopher crash his car? Did they mess with some wiring or cut a brake line?

The guilt returned in a gushing tsunami. If it *was* her fault for telling Christopher, and now this stalker was going to silence anyone with information, then there was no way she could tell anyone else. There was no way she could handle any more weight on her conscience. If something happened to Rachel . . . or her parents . . .

"No," she said again, staring down her reflection as if she were confronting the stalker. *"No! No! No!"*

Why had they chosen her? What made her so special? What had she done to deserve this?

She continued to hold a hard gaze at her mirrored self, her eyes streaked with black like some masked vigilante. She leaned in closer and pressed her forehead to the glass. Her heart beat wildly in her chest while her nostrils flared with deep and heavy exhales, creating foggy circles in the mirror that quickly dissipated.

It was there, face to face with herself, that she made a vow. She was going to have to walk amongst the shadows where the stalker crept and put a stop to them herself. She wasn't quite sure *exactly* what that entailed, but enough was enough. No one else was going to get hurt. Not if she could help it. She put her right hand against the mirror, her fingers splayed out, each one connected to its double. This was something she was going to have to do alone . . . or die trying.

Chapter 17

Determined as she was to step into the shadows and hunt her stalker down, Sabrina's first obstacle was trying to figure out *where* the so-called shadows began exactly. She had no clues. The stalker could be anyone. They could strike from anywhere. How was she supposed to lure them from their hiding place without causing harm to anyone else? How was she supposed to penetrate the darkness?

Sabrina was positive that if she asked her mom, there was certainly some sort of advice she would be able to give. She could picture her mom reaching into the imaginary bag in her head filled to the brim with sage wisdom and Hallmark-worthy phrases for every occasion and pulling out something like: *To drive away the darkness, you must be the light.*

Yeah, that's it! Sabrina sarcastically remarked in silence to herself. *Just be the light! Just shine that darkness away!*

It seemed obvious that whoever, or whatever, was lurking and watching her from a darkened distance only came for her when she was alone and vulnerable. She'd been helpless during each encounter so far, surprised in the school basement and asleep in her room. Sabrina was going to have to play this smart and be prepared. She wanted to draw the stalker out on her terms, not get caught in a trap or offer them an opportunity to get her.

For the time being, she clung close to people. She didn't wander the school halls alone or take solo trips to the bathroom. Despite Gina's protests, Sabrina stayed after school to oversee the cheering practices, baby doll in tow. If her parents went out or stayed late at work, she would get in her car and drive to a place with lots of people, somewhere public like the mall.

Yesterday she visited Christopher again. He looked the same, locked in stasis, the breathing tube protruding from his mouth. Sabrina sat with his family as long as the hospital would allow, holding hands with his mom and crying along with them.

Absence makes the heart grow fonder.

It wasn't a quote from her mom, per se, though Sabrina was almost certain she had likely said it to her at one point, but just one of those adages that seem to come pre-programmed in everyone's brains. She'd heard it a thousand times before, especially during the cheesy romance movies she and Rachel would watch, but the words seemed more poignant now than ever.

The amount of love she felt as she sat by his bedside surprised her. It was like nothing she'd ever felt before. She found herself missing so much about him. Obvious things like his hand caressing her back, grazing his hair with her fingers, his soft lips, cruising in his car, watching him play football, and cheering him on. But also, and perhaps most surprising to her, was she even found herself yearning for his stupid, immature comments and the moments where he would make her roll her eyes and contemplate the longevity of their relationship.

She missed *all* of Christopher and hoped, as she grieved alongside his family, that he would be able to feel the ripples of her love. Her picture-perfect Homecoming was in ruins at this point. Without Christopher, especially now that she was stuck with the baby doll, it was all pointless. A wish burned within her, though. Even if Christopher woke up today, she knew he was in no position to play football. He might even be done playing permanently. But if he *did* happen to open his eyes, at the very least, it was possible they could watch the homecoming game together. Something could still be salvaged from all of this. Her hand gripped his hospital bed railing tightly, willing it into existence with all her might.

Please wake up, Christopher. For your family. For me. Feel my love. Use it to wake up, please.

Before she knew it, Friday had rolled around, time for her sleepover. And how could she possibly forget? Rachel wasted no time in continually reminding her throughout the day, as though the plans were going to disappear from Sabrina's head like a magic trick.

If anything was to vanish from her mind, she wished it were the lingering thoughts of her stalker. She wanted to be able to enjoy the sleepover fully. To devote her full attention to Rachel and giggle and gossip with ease, without a shadow hanging over the entire evening or the need to keep an extra eye open and on alert.

Was she putting Rachel in serious danger by going to the sleepover? There was no way Sabrina could cancel now. Not with Rachel's bounding excitement. Plus, as she'd mentioned more than once, she'd *already* rented the tapes and stocked up on snacks.

Are they always watching and listening? Do they know about our plans? Are they going to follow me to her house?

Filled with trepidation, Sabrina mentally readied herself with the notion that girls' night might become a fight for their lives.

Chapter 18

"Wow!" Sabrina exclaimed, gawking at the snack-strewn counters in Rachel's kitchen. "Did you buy the whole store!?"

"C'mon, it's a girls' night. We *have* to pig out, otherwise it doesn't count."

There were all varieties of chips: regular, BBQ, sour cream and onion, and some cheese-flavored Doritos. There were chocolate chip cookies, Cosmic Brownies, bowls of licorice, and a giant bag of Sour Patch Kids, which just so happened to be Sabrina's favorite candy, particularly the yellow ones.

And maybe for a regular sleepover, all of that would be enough. But this wasn't a regular sleepover. Anyone who'd spent a night at *Casa de Stockworth* knew that, so Sabrina was not surprised in the slightest when Rachel continued to show off like she was a prize girl on *The Price Is Right*, opening up the fridge and freezer to present the cans of Pepsi, frozen pizza rolls and two *tubs*, not gallons, but tubs of vanilla and chocolate ice cream.

It was an absolute smorgasbord of sugar and happiness, and Sabrina was looking forward to digging in and doing her best to enjoy herself. It'd only been about ten minutes since she walked into the house, but she thought she was doing good so far.

"And that's not all . . ." Rachel announced, her voice trailing off for dramatic effect.

"Yeah?"

"I've also called in a large cheese and a large pepperoni pizza for delivery from Thompson Point House of Pizza. It should be here in ten minutes."

"*Ugh*, I hope Lawrence isn't the one bringing the pizzas here."

"That's right, he does work there, doesn't he?"

Sabrina bobbed her head up and down in big strokes. "He sure does. I saw him the other day when I went to visit Christopher for the first time, outside the hospital. Said he was delivering pizza to one of the doctors."

"And? Did he say or do something weird?"

"No, nothing out of his usual."

"He *is* a little creepy, but I think he's harmless. I mean, who wouldn't have a crush on you? You're gorgeous!"

Rachel tried to reach out and pat her friend's hair, but, almost instinctively, Sabrina dodged it, shifting her entire upper body to the side like some survival instinct.

"Are . . . are you okay?" Rachel asked, taken aback by the quick reaction.

Sabrina was equally as stunned. She'd already fixed her hair. Or at the very least, she'd made it so the chunk of missing hair was no longer noticeable by trimming and shortening everything. Still, her now fifteen-minute record of playing it cool, of trying not to be on edge, was over.

"Yeah . . . I'm okay. Sorry, just been a little jumpy lately . . . ever since Christopher's accident."

"I'm sorry."

"No, no, nothing to be sorry for. If anything, *I'm* sorry. Now I made things weird. Let's move on. How about movies? What did you end up picking for tapes?"

Rachel's eyes lit up. "Depends on what you're in the mood to watch. If you want romance, I picked up *Say Anything*." She grabbed at her chest and swooned, batting her lashes with a deep, yearning sigh. "If only a boy would stand outside my window with a boombox and play a meaningful song for me. I think I would melt."

"Seth hasn't done that yet?" Sabrina shot back with a grin, trying to slip back into her loose, fun self.

"Not funny," Rachel said with a playful shove.

"Careful for the baby!" Sabrina giggled, nodding at the baby doll in her arms.

"*Ah*, yes," Rachel replied with an air of sarcasm. "So you can hurt *my* heart, but *your* baby is off limits." Then she broke into a laugh.

"Hey!" Sabrina called out, still chuckling but slightly offended. "It's not *my* baby. It's . . . an assignment. It's my . . . homework."

"Well then, I hope your *homework* doesn't cry all night and ruin our sleepover." Rachel winked and dashed off to the living room to grab the rest of the videotapes she'd rented. "Come on, let me finish showing you what I got!"

"Okay, yeah, what else did you get?"

Rachel held a VHS tape box up in the air, once again presenting it like some game-show prize. "If you want action and pure sex appeal, I give you Tom Cruise in *Days of Thunder*."

Sabrina shook her head. Tom Cruise was a looker, all right, but a movie about car racing seemed really boring to her.

"No?" Rachel asked, picking up on Sabrina's body language instantly. "Okay, how about some horror, then? I got *Jason Goes To Hell: The Final Friday*! Look at that cover!"

Sabrina had to back up slightly as Rachel shoved the VHS box into her face. The cover depicted a strange, demonic-looking snake slithering through the eyeholes of a metallic hockey mask set against a backdrop of flames. It was certainly striking; she could give it that much. But if she had hardly been a horror movie fan before all of this, she was even less so now that it felt like she was living in one.

"Let's just stick with the romance," she said. The baby doll started to fuss in her arms. "After I feed my *homework*, of course."

Sabrina opened up the accessory bag and pulled out a bottle, shifting the baby onto its back to feed it. Rachel stared with intense intrigue as the doll's lips suctioned to the nipple of the bottle and began sucking the way a real baby would.

"Man, look at that little thing go!" she commented, eyes level with the doll's chin. "I can't believe it just drinks the bottle like that. Do you wonder what it feels like? Imagine if you had to breastfeed that thing?"

"*Ew*, Rachel! First of all, gross. Second of all, that would be impossible as I'd have to be *pregnant*, as in growing a *real* baby in my belly, to produce milk.

134

Now you've gone and made things weird, so I guess we're even?"

"Deal," Rachel said, extending her right hand. Sabrina accepted, balancing the baby with her left arm, and shook Rachel's hand. "No more weirdness."

"You're sure about that?" Sabrina eyed her with skepticism.

"Absolutely positive." Rachel made an invisible cross above her heart with her finger, but the wide smirk on her face said otherwise.

"Now, if you wouldn't mind grabbing some soap and a sponge and scrubbing my brain, I'd appreciate it. That image is going to haunt me for a long time."

A moment of quiet passed between the two girls as they sat on the couch. The reprieve in noise didn't last long. Soon, the hollow sounds of the baby's lips continually pulling on the nipple of the now-emptied bottle filled the room.

Smack.

Smack.

Sabrina pulled the bottle from its pulsing mouth. The doll continued the motion, suckling on nothing but air before it relaxed and started to close its eyes, settling down for a nap in her arms.

Before the quiet could creep back between them, the sound of car tires pulling into the driveway caught their attention. Rachel sprang from the couch and peeked through the blinds.

"*Ooh!* Our pizza is here!" she exclaimed. "And guess who's delivering it?"

Sabrina groaned. "I'll stay right here on the couch. You answer the door. And *don't* mention anything about me being here."

"What if he asks me what I'm doing with two whole pizzas?" Rachel whipped around, the blinds snapping back to formation, brandishing a mischievous smile.

"Tell him you're on a new diet, I don't care. But just remember, *I'm. Not. Here!*"

"Actually . . . won't he know you're here anyway? He *definitely* knows what kind of car you drive, and it's right there in my driveway."

Sabrina growled in frustration and sank into the couch cushions, as though she were a hermit crab retreating into its shell. Rachel laughed and perched herself by the front door, waiting for the doorbell to ring. She readied a wad of cash in her hand.

Now that it had fallen asleep, Sabrina placed the baby doll down onto one of the decorative pillows on the couch, eager to scarf down some pizza and get a break from tending to the plastic tot. She dreamed of the taste of gooey cheese and crispy pepperoni teasing her tongue.

Shouldn't the doorbell have rung already? What is taking so long? The driveway isn't that long. Just then, Rachel turned and shot Sabrina a look of impatience, confirming they were both thinking the same thing.

Sabrina's stomach suddenly growled, and she realized she hadn't eaten since earlier that morning, having once again skipped out on lunch to nourish the hungry baby doll.

After four painstakingly slow minutes had crawled by with no ring from the doorbell, the girls heard the screech of tires burning rubber in the driveway before peeling out and squealing down the road at what sounded like an incredibly high speed.

"What the . . ." Rachel whipped the front door open. Clouds of black exhaust hung at the end of her driveway like a strange fog delivered only to her address. A delicious aroma of hot cheese and sweet sauce wafted into her nostrils. Following the scent, her eyes fell upon the two pizza boxes neatly stacked by her feet on the porch.

"Are pizzas free tonight or something?" Rachel shrugged, stuffing the cash back into her pocket before reaching down to pick up the pizza boxes. Before closing the door, she gave one final glance down the driveway, but by now the fumes had dissipated and, aside from the tire tread markings stamped on the pavement, it was like no one had been there at all.

The second vial needs to be filled tonight. I can't wait much longer. It is growing impatient. The smile in the darkness. The teeth of eternal night. The jaws of the abyssal shadows. I fear if I don't move quickly, I won't get what I was promised. All this will have been for nothing.

No.

I can't have that.

The point of it all... the purpose... the reason... it must be realized. I refuse to accept that I have spilled blood and caused so much pain for nothing. No. I won't fail.

Your cute little blonde friend, Rachel Stockworth, is next up on the chopping block. I can see her right now, parading around her kitchen, showing off all the snacks and goodies she has bought for her sleepover with you.

I wish I could be an invisible set of eyes in the house. Or a fly on the wall. To hear your conversations. To swim in your youthful energy. To bask in one of your final pure moments with your friend. Oh, to be invited and get to be part of it all. To brush your hair and paint your nails and gorge on the endless bags of chips and cookies and spoonfeed you ice cream like a mama bird to her starved nestlings. To curl around furniture and gossip and listen to you spill your innermost secrets. To crawl into that space, to burrow in the warmth within your stomach, to witness the vessel from the inside.

How wonderous that would be.

Now to wait here in the bushes until you both eventually grow tired and fall asleep. Then I can sneak inside and stick to the shadows. A gag in her mouth, then a quick slice across the throat with my knife, and I'll fill the vial and vanish. Two down, one to go.

But, knowing how you girls can be, especially once they fill up on sugar and start chatting, that could be hours from now. The waiting pains me...

Hold on... there are headlights pulling into the driveway... Who's this? Was someone else invited to the sleepover? Oh, it's just someone delivering pizza. Wait a minute... is that Lawrence Watkins?

It is.

This is perfect! I've seen the way he eyes you, Sabrina. The way he lurks around, always on the edge, orbiting you like a distant moon. No, there can't be any of that. No distractions. I'm the only one that has eyes for you. The only one that needs you.

You are mine. You will give me what I desire.

I'm behind him before he even realizes what is happening. My left hand clasps over his mouth and nostrils. He drops the pizza boxes as his entire body rattles with fear. I tease him for a moment. My knife, firmly gripped in my right hand, presses into his neck. He winces, and I can hear him try to whimper, but it sounds all muffled.

"Don't move," I whisper. *"And don't you dare scream."*

His car idles at the end of the driveway. The headlights are too bright for my liking. I briefly let go of him, then bend down to grab the pizza boxes so I can set them on the porch.

You girls deserve your pizza. Enjoy it. Rachel gets to live for another day or two. Lucky her for ordering delivery.

I grab Lawrence by the throat and drag him back toward his car. He's quiet, like a good boy. The only sound is his shoes scraping against the paved driveway. A wave of weeks-old garbage, stale crumbs, and marijuana assaults me upon opening the driver's side door of his car.

My knife, as impatient as I am, zips across his throat before I shove his body into the vehicle. I rush inside and shut the door, grabbing a vial from my satchel. Then I fill it with the blood gushing out of the newly formed slit in his neck.

Two vials of blood collected. One more to go, and then I can get my prize. I can get what I've wanted for so long. The pain . . . I'm ready for the pain to cease. I'm so close I can almost taste it.

It will be very pleased.

Lawrence gurgles his last few breaths. Blood is all over the glove compartment, passenger seat, and gear shift. He really has made such a mess. I'll have to clean that later. For now, it's time for me to get out of here. Can't risk being seen. Not when I'm this close.

I shift the car into reverse and slam my foot onto the gas pedal, peeling out before zipping off down the street.

Enjoy your pizza and sleepover, Sabrina.

It will be your last.

The days are now numbered.

The pieces are almost in place.

The ritual will soon begin.

Prepare, my perfect vessel.

I await our reunion.

Rachel's blood will fill the third vial.

And I will offer my flesh to the smile in the darkness. To the grin that floats in the midnight shade. To the teeth of the ebony realm.

I will get what is owed to me.

Chapter 19

The early morning October sun assaulted Sabrina's eyes as she stepped out of Rachel's house and into the driveway. She put her free arm across her forehead to shield herself from the blaring rays that made the fallen leaves scattered across the front yard look like balls of fire. In her other arm, the baby doll, wriggling and screaming in her grasp.

So much for a sleepover, Sabrina thought with a roll of her eyes. She and Rachel had enjoyed some pizza and maybe twenty minutes of *Say Anything* before the doll had started its crying fit. Nothing seemed to console it. She fed it, she changed it, she rocked it, she sang to it, all to no avail. Rachel tried to help, grabbing the doll from Sabrina at one point, but that only made things worse. As instant as an allergic reaction, the second Rachel touched the baby, its cries rose in volume and intensity, transforming into an almost inhuman shriek as though she'd set the thing on fire.

"I'm so sorry," Sabrina had apologized over and over as tears of frustration and exhaustion leaked down her face.

"Nonsense," Rachel had said, swatting at the air. But the sentiment didn't last too long. Eventually, the incessant screaming broke her too. They'd had girls' nights filled with late-night crying sessions, but those were brought on by stupid boys and usually ended with hugs and smiles and a renewed sense of strength and empowerment between them. These tears were different. Spurred on by a relentless onslaught of headache-inducing cries and throat-shredding screams. And the kicker? The thing that truly drove Sabrina insane? The endurance test of madness she'd been subjected to was nothing more than a school project. She'd been pushed to the brink by a fake baby doll.

It was by far the worst girls' night she'd ever had, and she knew Rachel would agree with that statement.

I hate this thing! There's no way I can take another week of this. Nothing good has happened ever since it came into my life. I'm ready to toss it in a dumpster and take the F.

Sabrina kicked at a pebble in the driveway, knowing full well she would never actually do something like that. She'd never received a D in her life, never mind an F. She was bound to the baby for another six days.

She reached her car, but before she could open the door, the tire marks burned into the driveway caused her to turn her head. She thought back to last night, to the long wait, the pizza boxes left on the front porch, and the screeching tires as Lawrence made his exit.

He's such a weirdo.

She paused. A small glistening puddle next to the imprint of tire treads caught her eye. Was it oil? Had his car leaked some coolant as it burned rubber and tore out of the driveway? Or was it something else entirely? A sense that something was really wrong wrapped itself around her stomach, making her suddenly queasy.

Sabrina wasn't entirely sure why the puddle had piqued her curiosity or why it felt like her body was telling her to run, but as she approached to examine it further, the baby doll stopped crying entirely. The sudden quiet smashed into her like an out-of-control truck. She'd almost forgotten what it was like to *not* have a baby screaming uncontrollably in her ear.

As she gained her bearings and recovered from the whiplash caused by the baby doll's abrupt silence, she realized the puddle wasn't oil. There was no rainbow-like sheen to the fluid. She didn't think it was coolant either. It was too . . . red.

Is that blood?

The baby doll jiggled in her hold. Sabrina looked down to find a cheeky smile spread across its face. A chill tingled down her spine as she was instantly reminded of its expression while she had sat by Christopher's bedside at the hospital. How it had been cooing and smiling as it stared at his comatose body, almost like it was relishing in his misfortune.

It now brandished that same smile, its cheeks pink and puffy as its eyes locked onto the puddle. Her gut was telling her that the thing she didn't want to be true, in fact, was. Her stomach pulsed with intense pain, vomit threatening to burn its way up to her throat and out her mouth.

She crouched down, hovering over the red puddle, before reaching and touching the liquid with the tip of her left pointer finger. She knew she *shouldn't* do it, but her curiosity had hijacked the driver's seat, relegating her fear to the passenger side. A rusty, copper smell wafted off the crimson-brushed fingertip she ran beneath her nose.

It *was* a puddle of blood.

But . . . but . . .

The realization was like being force-fed a can of congealed dog food. Sabrina audibly gagged, choking on her own spit and, without knowing what else to do with it, wiped the blood on her pants.

Whose blood was it? And why was it there in Rachel's driveway? Was it Lawrence's? Had he somehow cut himself? Is that why he sped out of here? What if . . . what if something bad happened to him?

Her curiosity had finished its cruise, slinking away into the backseat so fear could resume its command of the wheel. If it *was* Lawrence's blood and if something terrible did happen to him, well, now some of that was smudged on her pants.

Why did I do that? Sabrina scolded herself. *That was really stupid.*

The baby doll started smacking its lips in the same way it would when it wanted a bottle, only this time with a feverish intensity Sabrina had never seen it display before. Its mouth pulsed rapidly, like an image on a VHS tape being fast-forwarded. It thrashed its arms and legs, beating them against Sabrina's side. She was alarmed at the impact of its little hands and feet.

And then a searing pain shot through her arm.

The doll had bitten her.

She yelped and flung the baby from her arms. It

flipped through the air and then landed with a *thud* on the driveway, mere feet from the puddle of blood.

Sabrina examined her arm. A bright pink circle had formed on her skin where the baby doll had chomped down. She definitely didn't recall anything from Ms. Pike's rundown about it being able to bite. How did it have that much strength to leave a mark like that and inflict pain? It didn't even have any teeth!

I'm giving it back, Sabrina decided. *Come Monday, I'm marching right into Ms. Pike's class and tossing it right on her desk. Something is wrong with this thing. I'll offer to write an essay or do some extra credit work, but I'm done with this assignment.*

She sighed and was about to scoop it back up, but what she saw caused her entire body to freeze in place.

The doll had steadied itself on its hands and knees and was crawling toward the puddle, lips still smacking together like a machine on the fritz. It wore a look of determination, its eyes focused solely on the blood as it scurried along the asphalt.

To her utter horror, once it reached the edge of the stain in the driveway, she watched it flop down into the puddle face-first as though its plastic arms and legs had suddenly turned to liquid. Sabrina cringed at the wet, sickening *slurps* as the baby doll, with its face pressed down into the crimson, started suckling the blood.

It screeched in protest as Sabrina grabbed its leg and lifted it away from the puddle. It twisted and turned, belting out banshee screams, but she held firm around its ankle. Blood was smeared across its face like cake frosting on a baby's first birthday.

"What the hell is *wrong* with you!?" Sabrina demanded, as if the doll could answer.

And while it didn't verbally respond, it did furrow its brows and cast a mean, deadly glare at her, made all the more terrifying by the blood painted on its face. Flustered with fear, Sabrina opened her car door and tossed the baby doll inside. It hit the passenger seat, then rolled and bounced off, landing on the floor in a tempered fit.

She ignored it, closing the door, buckling herself in, and starting the car before backing out of the driveway. She turned up the radio to drown out the doll's incessant noise. It made a few attempts to crawl, but each time Sabrina noticed it move out of the corner of her eye, she would sharply cut the wheel, causing it to lose all balance. After landing on its back, it seemed to give up and resigned to crying and flailing on the floor of the car.

Every so often, as Sabrina did her best to remain focused on the road and get home as quickly as possible, in between its shrill howls, the baby doll would stutter as if trying to sound out a word.

Road, road, road, pay attention to the road played out in her mind like a jingle on a radio commercial. She slowed at the intersection between Emerson and Squall Street and, after looking both ways, made a prompt left turn without coming to a full, complete stop.

Eyes on the road keeps the eyes in your head is what her mom loved to say when Sabrina had been learning to drive. With that memory now floating up to the surface, the song in her head changed. The sounds of old-time swing music, punctuated by trumpets and horns, swelled around her as a static, disembodied female voice sang: *eyes on the road keeps the eyes in your head*.

Her dad's favorite piece of driving advice had always been *safety doesn't happen by accident*. This, of course, he always offered up with a wink and that toothy grin of his. It didn't, however, seem to lend itself to a song. Her mom's mantra continued to swell around her like a dusty memory from some long-forgotten '30s jazz club.

"Bl, bl, bl . . ."

The baby's sudden babbling ushered her parents' words to the forgotten, cobweb-filled recesses of her brain.

"Blah, blah, blah . . ."

Sabrina could pretend she wasn't hearing it all she wanted, but as the chatter continued to spew forth from its pursed lips, it was growing more impossible to ignore the fact that a word was forming. It kept trying, forcing the word to roll off from the tip of its tongue.

The roof of her house was within her sight now. In less than a minute, she would whip into her driveway, and then she could . . . what? What was her plan with the baby? What was she going to do all weekend until Monday rolled around?

That was when the word presented itself, clear and unmistakable, bursting out into the car like the baby alien creature in that movie Rachel had forced her to watch last summer.

"*Blood*."

Now in her driveway, Sabrina slammed her foot on the brake, shifted into park, and glanced over at the baby doll. It stared up at her from the floor of the car, its face splattered and smeared in red blotches. It smiled as if it were proud. Then, it repeated the word over and over.

"Blood. Blood. Blood."

Chapter 20

Monday morning, Sabrina pulled into the school parking lot with determination. The baby doll lay on its back in the passenger seat, open-mouthed but quiet. She parked her car in her usual spot, slipped her backpack over her shoulders, then grabbed it by its wrist, holding it away from her as if it were a smelly piece of garbage.

The rest of the weekend had dragged, but was, for the most part, uneventful. Sabrina had come home and snuck past her parents, not wanting them to see the doll and have to explain the red stains on its face. She cleaned the blood with a wet facecloth, scrubbing hard with a hateful intensity, hoping, somehow, the doll would *feel* it. She had hesitated around its mouth, expecting another bite or some form of retaliation, but surprisingly, it did nothing. When she pulled the cloth away, it was like staring at a brand new baby doll. Sparkly and new, factory fresh, without one speck of blood.

From that point on, she'd done the bare minimum. Feeding the baby with its bottles when it cried out in hunger and occasionally changing its diaper, though not nearly as often as she normally would.

Other than that, Sabrina was hands-off, completely detached.

Yesterday she visited Christopher again, but decided to leave the baby at home. It was napping when she placed it in a shoe box and tucked it beneath her bed. The normal guilt that would have plagued her for doing such a thing, even if it was only a doll, was absent. She thought only of Christopher. Poor, sweet Christopher.

Without the doll stuck to her like an unwanted growth, Sabrina was able to focus all her attention and energy on Christopher. There hadn't been any changes since she'd last seen him. The breathing tube was still down his throat. A jungle of wires and machinery still surrounded his hospital bed. Everything was still day by day.

She'd returned home feeling drained, like she had poured all the love she could into that room. Hoping it was enough to reach Christopher. To help wake him up from the shadowed realm he'd been banished to. When she reached her bedroom, ready to wrap herself in the comfort of her blankets and pillows, the baby doll was waiting for her, sitting upright atop her comforter. On the floor by the edge of her bed, spread out like an explosion of party confetti, was the shoe box torn to shreds.

All that was going to end now. Due to the rotating schedule, Ms. Pike's class just so happened to be Sabrina's first period. Not that it would have stopped her from barging into her classroom anyway once the bell rang.

"I don't want this *thing* anymore," Sabrina said,

slamming the baby doll onto Ms. Pike's desk. It let out a startled whimper.

"Ms. Quinn, what are you talking about?" Ms. Pike asked, her eyes quickly darting between Sabrina and the baby doll.

"There's something *wrong* with it."

Ms. Pike's eyes widened with concern. "Wrong? What do you mean wrong? This model is top of the line. It was purchased brand new. You were the first student to have it. There shouldn't be any issues at all."

"Ms. Pike, I get that and all but..." Sabrina hesitated. Was she really going to say it? Was she going to tell her teacher the baby had crawled across a driveway to plant its face in a puddle of blood? That it had bitten her? That it had torn its way out of a shoebox? Or that it always seemed to smile at Christopher?

"But what?"

"I... I don't know how to say this without sounding crazy, but there are things that have happened... things the doll has done that I can't explain. Things it should *not* be able to do. It... it bit me. And it... it drank from a puddle of blood." Sabrina leaned forward and lowered her voice, not wanting anyone else to hear her.

Too late.

"*Aw*, what's the matter? Little Miss Perfect can't handle a baby, *huh?*" Of course, Gina had to butt in. She snorted and chuckled to herself.

"Thank you, Gina, but this doesn't concern you," Ms. Pike scolded, responding before Sabrina even had a chance to react. "Now, what were you saying? The doll bit you?"

"It did!" Sabrina pulled up the sleeve on her sweater and pointed, but the pink mark left by the bite was gone. Her skin was as perfect as ever, soft and white, without so much as a blemish or freckle. Realizing that and seeing the look of disbelief on Ms. Pike's face, she hastily tugged her sleeve back down, feeling instantly foolish.

"Sabrina . . ."

"No! Ms. Pike, listen. I *know* how this sounds, trust me. But I'm not making it up. It bit me! Then it started drinking blood!"

"Whose blood?"

"I don't know!"

An elated smile blossomed on Ms. Pike's face. Sabrina had seen it before. It was the same smile that had bloomed on the doll's face in the hospital.

"Why . . . Why are you smiling?"

"Because I see what's going on here, and I'm amazed to see this project working even more brilliantly than I imagined."

Sabrina's mouth fell open.

What is she talking about?

"Let me ask you a few things. Are you feeling overwhelmed? Possibly a bit hopeless? Does it seem like this project might never end? Your sleep schedule is all out of whack, isn't it? Is the baby keeping you up at night? It must be, look at those dark circles under your eyes. You poor thing."

"Yes, it keeps me up at night *sometimes*, but that's not what I'm complaining about," Sabrina tried. But something in Ms. Pike's eyes told her it didn't matter what she said.

"Do you not feel like your usual self anymore now that you have a baby in tow? Does it upset you that you no longer have time for the things you once had time for? Is there resentment growing within you? I can see it on your face. And you know what? It's all perfectly normal. Plenty of women go through the same thing."

"*Huh?*"

"Don't you see?" Ms. Pike said, reaching across her desk to grab Sabrina by the wrists. "You're experiencing the effects of postpartum depression."

"What?" She pulled her arms away from Ms. Pike's grasp and took a step backward. On the desk, the doll cooed and kicked its feet. "How is that even possible? I *never* had a baby! That thing is just a doll!"

"That's the beauty!" Ms. Pike exclaimed. "You don't have to. It's about the connection. This doll has unlocked the motherly instincts within, and your body and mind are stressed. And how could you not be? There's been so much disruption in your life. I *know* you are missing your cheerleading, and this has been cutting into your homecoming festivities, and it's absolutely terrible what happened to your boyfriend. But that's what this project is all about. Things are *always* going to be happening, good and bad. You see now how truly difficult it can be to juggle so many things, all while trying to take care of a little baby."

You forgot to mention being stalked this entire time. Sabrina wanted to speak but was stunned into silence. Was Ms. Pike for real? Postpartum depression? From a stupid, plastic doll?

"It makes perfect sense why you came in here wanting to give it up. Saying the baby bit you and that it . . . drank blood? Is that what you said? That's the depression talking. It's just your brain making things up and *convincing* you that you would be better off without the baby."

But I would be better off without the baby! If I hadn't been the first one chosen, then everything would be the way it should. I bet Christopher would have never even had his accident. I'd be on the sidelines of the homecoming game, cheering him on, and he'd be on the field scoring touchdowns and making the crowd go wild. It would be the senior year I've dreamed of. The senior year I'm supposed to be having.

"I *don't* have postpartum depression!" Sabrina cried out. Her outburst drew the attention of the entire class. All eyes were on her now. Especially Gina, grinning with wide-eyed intrigue.

"It's nothing to be ashamed of," Ms. Pike replied. "You can't just *give up*. You're almost done! After today, you only have four days left."

"I don't care," Sabrina returned. Her eyes burned with frustration. *Please don't cry. Please don't cry.* That was the last thing she needed. She was supposed to be strong. To be a leader in the school. If Gina saw that, she'd never hear the end of it. "I don't care about the grade anymore. You're not hearing me, Ms. Pike. There's something wrong with that thing. It's like it's defective or possessed or something."

"What do you mean you don't care about the grade anymore? That's not like you."

"How would you know what I'm like? You haven't seen me for years."

"But I knew you from before, and I've seen your academic records. You're not just the top of your class but the top of the entire school, Sabrina. Failing is simply not in your DNA. Anyone can see that. Face it, you're pretty much *perfect*."

Warmth spread across Sabrina's cheeks as though she were back at the bonfire. She didn't need a mirror to know her cheeks were flushed as pink as the balm glistening off Gina's lips. The weight of everyone's eyes pressed on her like a crushing wall of concrete.

"You can't quit, Sabrina. I refuse to let you," Ms. Pike said. She slid the doll toward the edge of the desk. "Take the baby and finish up. It's only another four days."

"*Oh*, mighty leader, you're not, like, really gonna quit, are you? What kind of example would that be, especially to all the future young moms that might be looking up to you?" Gina blurted out with a snicker.

Sabrina didn't turn around. The tears were already dripping down her face. With her head hung low in defeat, she plucked the baby doll from Ms. Pike's desk and briskly walked out of the classroom.

Four more days.

It felt more like a hundred-year prison sentence.

On top of all that, the stalker was still out there somewhere. Watching. Waiting.

As if in response, the baby doll let out a laugh that bounced off the locker doors and swelled within the empty hallway.

Chapter 21

"Gina is driving me absolutely insane," Rachel complained before slurping up the last of her strawberry milkshake. She and Sabrina both had a rough Monday, and it seemed like a trip to the mall for some sugary treats and maybe a new outfit was the perfect remedy.

"Want to trade for this thing?" Sabrina asked, pointing to the doll resting atop the food court table. "You can take care of the baby, and I'll work on the homecoming decorations. I'll gladly put up with Gina's crap instead."

"Are you sure about that?" Rachel asked, tilting her head with a thin-lipped smile.

"Absolutely. Gina is just a bigger baby, but at least I wouldn't have to change her diapers." Both girls let loose in a fit of giggles at this.

"For real, though, she's *demanding* we show up each night this week after dinner to get everything done. You should see all the changes she's made. Fern quit last week, and Jenny is not far behind her. I'm practically the last still on the committee. I'm sure Gina would just love it if I left. Then she could get *all* the glory."

"I can only imagine. If she had it her way, we'd be cheering for the Thompson Point Gina Applegates!"

"*Oh*, it would be worse than that," Rachel said with a shudder at the thought. She tapped her empty milkshake cup against the table and then stood up. "Come on, let's go check out Wet Seal and try on some clothes. At least Gina can't dictate what I wear . . . for now."

Rachel tossed her cup into the nearest trash can and let out a celebratory "*Woo!*" when it bounced off the rim and landed inside. Sabrina gave an enthusiastic round of applause before swiping the baby doll from the table and joining her friend to venture off to the clothing store.

The mall was fairly dead, and as they strolled beneath the long strips of neon lights that bordered the main walkway, Sabrina couldn't help but feel like they were the only ones there. Almost as though they were in some private dreamworld, as if the mall itself knew they needed a respite from the chaos of their lives and the noise of other people. A quiet place to eat, shop, and feel normal for even one hour. Even the baby doll seemed to be in on it, sleeping peacefully in Sabrina's arms.

They entered Wet Seal and were instantly greeted by the sole employee of the store, a petite blonde, a few years older than them. She made a beeline for the girls, approaching with a beaming mouth full of teeth.

"Welcome, girls! Can I help you find anything today?" She had a great customer service voice, bright and cheery, but Sabrina could tell it was a façade.

"Just poking around," Rachel answered, rushing past to look at a rack of dresses.

"Well, my name is Destiny," she pointed at the nametag pinned to her shirt, "I'll just be over there by the register if you girls need anything."

"Thank you," Sabrina said.

An Ace of Base song played from the store's music system at a moderate volume, low enough that the girls could chatter and gawk at the clothes without having to shout, but loud enough to provide atmosphere and give them something to nod their heads to as they perused the racks. Sabrina found herself silently mouthing along to the words and bobbing her head up and down as she pawed through a shelf of folded graphic tees, only to pause when the chorus hit and she realized it said *"all that she wants is another baby."*

Yeah, right, Sabrina smirked. She knew the song wasn't referring to an actual baby, but given the circumstances of the last week and the horrors the baby doll had put her through, it was enough to cease her lip-synching. Still, she couldn't deny the beat and continued to bop along to the music as she plucked a couple of the shirts to try on in the fitting room.

She peered over at Rachel, whose face was buried behind the mountain of clothes in her arms, her blonde hair poking out the top like a snowcap at the peak.

"Are you going to buy *all* of those?" Sabrina asked.

"No," Rachel answered, her voice muffled by the clothes. "But a girl's gotta have options, right?"

"There is such a thing as *too* many options! Are you still looking, or are you ready to try these on?"

"I'm ready, I just have to pee first. You go on ahead. I'm going to leave these with Destiny, and I'll meet you back by the fitting rooms."

"Sounds good."

Since they were the only ones in the store, Sabrina had her choice of the five available fitting rooms. The first one, being handicapped-accessible, was larger than the others. She opted to leave that one for Rachel, knowing she had bundled half the store into her arms. She entered the second stall, closed the door, and then placed the still sleeping infant down onto the small bench inside.

Sabrina placed her selections beside the baby, careful not to disturb it. A temper tantrum was the last thing she needed right now. All she wanted was a fun afternoon at the mall with her best friend. To laugh and try on clothes and maybe buy a new outfit and feel sexy and cool and all the things she used to feel before everything went so wrong.

As she was about to try the first shirt on, the music in the store stopped. A dense and sudden silence blanketed Sabrina like a snow squall. She dropped the shirt and listened. As far as she could tell, there was no movement in the store. She couldn't hear any footsteps or the squeaking of hangers being shuffled on the clothing racks or the sunny fakeness of Destiny's voice.

Then the speakers crackled, and it made Sabrina jump with a gasp. She clutched her chest and breathed slowly, trying to ease her startled heart. A new song started to play, but the volume was much louder than before. Was Destiny fiddling around with the dials on the music system? Is that what had caused the unexpected surge of quiet? Had she turned up the music on purpose?

The music was almost too loud for her to think. Muted guitars and a steady drumbeat rang in her ears. Sabrina knew this song. Her parents played it all the time. It was a song from their favorite band, "Every Breath You Take" by The Police.

The singer's voice crooned through the speakers: *"Every breath you take . . ."* She'd heard the song probably a thousand times and always thought of it as a nice love song, but there in the fitting room, as the music pounded like a late-night club, she couldn't help but notice a sinister tone to it. Her heart thundered just as loudly against her ribcage. The walls seemed to close in around her.

A new voice emerged, cutting through the song like a knife through a birthday cake. It too was singing, breathy, almost whisper-like, but full-bodied and defined. The voice was right outside the fitting room door.

"You are my sunshine, my only sunshine, you make me happy, when skies are gray . . ."

Sabrina held her breath and slowly backed up against the far wall. Had this been a trap the whole time? Was Destiny the stalker? No, Sabrina realized, there's no way. They'd never even met. She was a twenty-something mall employee, likely working there while she got through college. Why would she be stalking a high school senior? It didn't matter. Whoever it was, they were here, and they had her trapped in the fitting room with nowhere to go.

"You'll never know dear, how much I love you, please don't take my sunshine away . . ."

Sabrina briefly glanced around, scanning the small space for any sort of weapon she could use. *Of course,* she had only grabbed a few folded shirts, so there were no hangers handy. Other than that, all she noticed was the bench. She knelt and tried to lift it as a test, but it was too heavy. There was no way she'd be able to hoist it up and throw it at her assailant. She'd left the accessory bag in her car, silently praying she wouldn't need it and the doll would let her shop in peace. Somehow, the doll had heeded her wish. It still was. Amidst all the noise and chaos, it continued to lie peacefully on the bench, eyes shut in a cozy synthetic slumber.

If it really came down to it, she could always just grab the baby doll by the leg and smash it into the stalker's face to make her escape.

The fitting room door rattled, and Sabrina turned to see a gloved hand reaching through the open slit, its black leather-clad fingers clasping the underside edge.

Rachel! Where are you!? Help me! Sabrina screamed internally.

The hand was wrenching on the door now. She had to do something. The door was far less sturdy than the ones in the school bathrooms, made from cheap particleboard. It wouldn't be long until it snapped off its hinges, and the shadows on the other side would rush in to claim her.

She stood and reached into her pocket, suddenly remembering the pen she had tucked away after her first-period class. She pulled it out and removed the cap, preparing herself for what was to come next.

She had to be brave.

"*Fierce*," she chanted under her breath. "You need to be fierce."

"*I'll be watching you . . . I'll be watch . . .*"

The music cut out again. The door stopped rattling. The invading hand disappeared. Sabrina steadied the pen in her grasp, raising it above her head.

"*Tonight,*" the voice whispered. "*I can't wait anymore.*"

"*No!*" Sabrina screamed, quickly unlocking and kicking open the door without any further hesitation. In a blind fury, she brought the pen down, plunging it into the stalker's shoulder.

"*Ahhhhh!* Sabrina!"

She pulled the pen back, ready to strike again, when her vision returned, and Sabrina realized it wasn't her mysterious stalker she had stabbed. *It was Rachel.* A thin line of blood ran down her arm from the pen's entry wound.

Hearing the screams, Destiny ran over to see what was going on, only to start screaming herself upon seeing Rachel bleeding on the floor with Sabrina standing over her, brandishing a pen.

"I'm calling security!" she yelled out, before running off through the employee-only door adjacent to the fitting rooms.

"Why'd you stab me!?" Rachel cried. "What's going on?"

Sabrina had no words. She remained rooted in place with her hand over her mouth, paralyzed with shock and bewilderment. Where had the stalker gone? How had they disappeared so quickly? And then an even worse thought crept into the forefront.

Had she imagined it? Was her fear and paranoia making her absolutely crazy?

Before any more questions could blast through her brainwaves, a rustling from behind captured Sabrina's attention, momentarily breaking her frozen stance. Whipping her head toward the fitting room, she saw it was the baby doll lowering itself from the bench. It plopped down onto the floor, landing on its rear end before flipping over to crawl on its hands and knees. It scuttled forward like a cockroach escaping the bright beam of a flashlight.

"*Blood. Blood. Blood,*" it said in a soft, robotic tone, with its eyes focused solely on Rachel.

With pure panic surging through her veins, Sabrina dropped the pen and scooped the baby doll into her arms like a fumbled football.

"I'm sorry!" she said to Rachel as she rushed past. "Please forgive me, I'm so sorry!"

"Wait! Sabrina, don't leave me!"

"I'm sorry!" she shouted once more before zipping out of the store.

Running toward the end of the mall where she'd parked her car, with the bloodthirsty baby tucked in the crook of her arm, Sabrina was more like one of the Thompson Point Tigers players than a cheerleader. She bolted past store after store, eyes zeroed in on the exit doors as if they were goal posts. Without slowing down or losing momentum, she burst through the doors and hightailed it in the direction of her car.

"*Blood. Blood. Blood,*" the baby continued to chant as it twisted and turned in her grasp.

Her legs throbbed with pain, but she finally made

it to her car, tearing the door open and hurling the baby onto the passenger seat. Then, completely out of breath, she turned the key, shifted into drive, and slammed her foot onto the gas pedal.

The car peeled out of the lot with squealing tires and burning smoke, and within seconds, the mall was in her rearview, growing smaller and smaller as the distance increased until it disappeared entirely. At some point, the baby doll had settled, no longer calling out for blood.

Sabrina flicked her blinker on and pulled her car to the side of the road. She closed her eyes and tried to slow her heart rate, stretching back in her seat while taking long, calming breaths in through her nose, holding, and then exhaling through her mouth. She had escaped, for now anyway, but she knew this temporary reprieve wouldn't last long.

What she couldn't escape were the parting words of her stalker. The message whispered just before she mistakenly stabbed her best friend.

Tonight. I can't wait anymore.

Can't wait for what? Sabrina wondered with a shudder.

To kill her?

Chapter 22

Sabrina hesitated for what must have been the hundredth time before she finally grabbed the phone from her bedside table and began to dial Rachel's number. Her fingers trembled as she pressed the buttons. The guilt tore her apart. What had started as a pit in her stomach now enveloped her entire body, covering her like a heavy blanket. She placed the phone up to her ear as it started ringing and waited, hoping Rachel would answer. That she would accept her apology.

"Hello?"

"Rachel!" Sabrina cried, almost choking on tears. "How ... how are you doing? I ... I just wanted to call and tell you how sorry I am. I didn't mean to ... and the way I bolted and just left you there ... I ... I can explain."

"I'm okay, it was just a poke, really. Enough to make me bleed a little, but still. The medical crew at the mall came and checked me out. No major damage. Do you mind telling me *what* that was all about, though? When you burst through that door ... your eyes ... they weren't yours. You looked ... borderline *possessed!* You really scared me."

Sabrina sniffled and sighed. "I'm so sorry. Listen, Rachel, there's something I have to tell you. I probably should have told you a while ago, but . . . I didn't want to put you in danger."

"Danger? What do you mean by that?"

Before she could explain, the baby doll began to shake on the bed beside her. The tremors emanating from its body traveled across the sheets, vibrating her entire mattress. It lifted its head and started to cry, sending a burst of high-pitched shrieks into the room that pierced through the phone. On the other end, Rachel pulled the receiver away from her ear.

"*Shh, shh, shh*, not now," Sabrina pleaded, reaching over to rub her hand across the baby doll's back. It wasn't helping. If anything, it only agitated things more. She tried to remind herself that there were only four days left with the baby, but she wasn't sure her patience, which was now as thin as a single strand of hair, would make it. Grabbing one of her pillows in frustration, she covered the doll with it in an attempt to muffle its screams. Then she swung her legs off the bed and retreated as far away as the phone cord would allow.

"Sorry," Sabrina said. "That thing is truly going to drive me insane."

"Tell me about this danger," Rachel replied. "Are you okay?"

"*Someone* is stalking me."

"Stalking you? Like what, leaving you love notes in your locker? Calling you at night and breathing into the phone?"

"Much more than that."

The doll's cries shifted into horrific growls, rising

in volume as if the pillow weren't there at all. Sabrina blocked her open ear with her free hand, doing her best to ignore the monstrous sounds coming from her bed.

"Sorry..."

"What is that *noise*? Is that the baby?"

"Yes." Sabrina grumbled, brimming with irritation.

"*Jeez*," Rachel said. "They built that thing with a super set of lungs, *huh?*"

"It's not right. Something is wrong with this damn doll! Have you ever even heard a normal baby screech like that?"

"No..." Rachel bit her lip as she contemplated for a moment. "But then again, I'm not really around *any* babies at all, really, so I don't have much to compare to."

Sabrina tried to retreat farther away but stopped when she heard the phone's cradle smash onto the floor. The growls grew louder, becoming a swirling vortex of painful noise. Rachel said something, but all Sabrina heard was a faint, garbled semblance of a voice. There was no competing with the doll now. It had become a megaphone of searing cries and bellowing shrieks, filling her bedroom with inhuman sounds.

She could hardly think. Her eyes flashed with the pain of a thousand headaches. Was there such a thing as postpartum rage? Because that's what Sabrina felt now. Pure, animalistic rage with her blood boiling and her head about to explode.

Why is it doing this? That thing has never thrown a tantrum this bad. Why won't it SHUT UP!?

"...can...hear..." Rachel's voice attempted to

break through, but it was like a hollow shout trapped in a tin can, as indistinguishable as static on the radio.

"What!?" Sabrina yelled, desperate to resume contact with her friend. "I'm sorry! I can't hear you!"

"... meet me at ... school ... with Homecoming ..."

Fragments were coming to Sabrina's ears. Small bits materializing in between the borderline demonic sounds belting from the baby doll's mouth.

"*Huh?*" Sabrina yelled into the receiver, hoping Rachel could at least hear her. "Meet you at school? Is that what you said? Why?"

"Gina ... cracking the whip ... me crazy ... emember?"

A bubble of a memory arose in Sabrina's head. She recalled Rachel mentioning that Gina was making insane demands for the homecoming committee and forcing them to come in after school hours to ensure all the decorations were to her specifications. The memory burst as quickly as it came, popped by the piercing screams spewing from the doll like a torrent of knives.

"You want me to meet you at the school?" Sabrina asked, trying to match the baby's volume and intensity.

"... now ... me in gymnasium ... help me ... you owe me ..."

"You're right. I *do* owe you, after the stabbing and all. I'll head out in a few. See you in the gymnasium." She hoped that was what Rachel had been trying to say. That's what she had been able to piece together with the sparse amount of words she'd been able to make out.

"See you soon!" Sabrina said before hanging up the phone and turning her attention to the baby doll, ready to silence it by any means necessary.

"Shut up! *Shut up! Shut! Up!*"

It was still buried beneath her pillow. She was surprised there weren't blue lights flashing and police sirens whooping out in front of her house. Her parents weren't home, but with the way the baby was screaming, she found it hard to believe someone in the neighborhood hadn't called in an attempted murder yet.

Sabrina stormed over and removed the pillow, revealing the little terror squirming about on top of her comforter. Its face had changed entirely. Its thin baby lips turned up in a snarl, and its eyes narrowed in anger, like someone scorned by their best friend. And the howling! With the pillow gone, the screams were even louder. If she didn't get it quiet quickly, someone was *surely* going to call the cops.

At this point, there was only one way she was going to accomplish that. It would mean a failing grade, of course. But Sabrina was beyond caring about that. Her grades were one of the furthest things from her mind at the moment. And even so, was *one* failed project really going to drag her GPA that drastically?

She tore open her bedroom door and flew to the kitchen. The baby doll's fiendish caterwauling spilled out of the open doorway and seemed to follow Sabrina, wafting behind her and filling up the empty space in the rooms of her house. She was surrounded by a cacophony, pushing through a fog of sound as she scrounged through the various drawers in the kitchen, looking for the screwdriver she knew was in there somewhere.

"C'mon, c'mon!" she pleaded, moving aside pens, spare batteries, and hundreds of loose elastic bands. Finally, tucked in the back corner of the third drawer she tried, her fingers felt the handle. She pulled out the screwdriver, holding it up in front of her face like some treasured object from a video game before rushing back to her bedroom.

Sabrina whisked toward the baby doll as it continued its tumultuous onslaught, the rope of her sanity attached only by mere threads now. She turned the flailing fleshy thing onto its belly and undid its diaper to expose the battery compartment door that was its rear end.

One screw, she thought, examining the task ahead. *One measly screw, and I never have to hear this thing scream again.*

She moved swiftly, fitting the head of the screwdriver into the grooves and then twisting until it came loose. Prying open the little door, Sabrina popped the two heavy-duty D sized batteries out. The crying, screaming, bellowing—whatever it was—ceased, and the baby doll's arms and legs stopped moving.

Sabrina expelled a breath of relief and flopped onto her pillow. She closed her eyes and took in the silence, let it fall around her like gentle snow delicately covering her in white. The doll could stay here while she met up with Rachel at the school.

She glanced at her alarm clock and saw it was nearing 6:30 PM. The thought of a baby-free evening spent painting and decorating with her best friend put a smile on her face. It would be like getting a taste of how things *should* have been. A stroll through the reality that the wretched doll had stolen from her.

Sabrina sat up and swung her legs off the side of the bed, the batteries still clutched tight in her palm. She stood and slipped them into her pocket. *Good luck without these*, she taunted, as if the baby doll were going to get up, find them, and put them back in itself.

A sweet, tender laugh sliced through the mute air.

Sabrina, nearly at her bedroom door with her fingers hovering above the knob, froze in place. She turned, slowly and carefully, wishing what she'd just heard wasn't real.

But it was.

The naked doll was standing up on her bed, the battery compartment still open and visible in the gap between its legs. It let out a high-pitched squeal, followed by a series of giggles as if Sabrina had just made a funny face or voiced a stuffed animal in a goofy way.

"*Oh*, hell no," Sabrina said, taking a few steps back. The bulge of the batteries in her pocket seemed to swell, a reminder of the impossible becoming possible before her very eyes.

Whatever you are, you're going back where you belong.

Her body bolted into action, swiping her backpack off the floor and then reaching across her bed to grab the baby doll. She plucked it by its feet, stuffing it into the backpack and then zipping it shut. This was Ms. Pike's problem now. She would meet Rachel in the gymnasium, and together they could run it down and dump the baby off in her classroom.

On her way through the kitchen, as the baby

laughed from the darkened confines of her backpack, Sabrina paused. The warning—*no*, the threat—from her stalker pinged in her brain like an alarm.

Tonight. I can't wait anymore.

Wrenching open the utensil drawer once more, she sifted through the unorganized mess until she found the Swiss Army knife. Ignoring all the other attached tools, she pulled out the blade portion. It glinted in the pale light from the stove hood, almost like a wink that said *I got your back*. Sabrina certainly hoped so. She tossed the hefty batteries into the drawer and then tucked the knife into her now emptied pocket. This time, she wasn't going to be trapped. She was prepared to fight back.

Chapter 23

As Sabrina pulled into the Thompson Point High parking lot, another car was leaving. The vehicle slowed and observed her car before speeding off, blazing in a pink blur down the twisting road leading out of the school. The color was all she needed to know exactly who it was.

Gina.

The '93 Pontiac Firebird, sparkling with a bratty, bubblegum pink custom paint job, had been her sixteenth birthday present from her parents. Gina had made sure to show it off every chance she could, *especially* at the football games. She'd even tried to offer Christopher a ride in it one afternoon, but he had refused.

Sabrina smirked as she pulled her car along the curb outside the gymnasium and put it in park. Gina could flex with her stupid, pink car all she wanted, but she still didn't have Christopher *or* the title of head cheerleader. And she *definitely* wasn't valedictorian, not even close.

At least she's leaving, so I don't have to deal with her. Rachel and I can work in peace ... after we get rid of this baby, of course.

Speaking of the baby, it was oddly quiet and had been for most of the ride over. It laughed occasionally but grew quieter the closer she got to the school. Her backpack sat on the passenger seat, steady and still as a normal bag should. Was it plotting something, or had it simply settled into the darkness, resigned to the fact that it was imprisoned?

Sabrina grabbed the pack by its handle, not wanting to wear it across her back just in case the baby doll did have some sort of plan or bit through the material. It had already bitten her once, and though she was now aware that it could operate without the aid of batteries, she had no idea what its powers were exactly or what force was giving it life. She extended her arm, holding the backpack as far away from her as she could. Keeping as much distance as possible between her and the baby doll seemed like the most logical plan.

Crisp leaves crunched beneath her feet as she hurried down the paved walkway toward the gymnasium. Gina's vision for Homecoming was already in full swing. Bales of hay lined the edge of the school building, topped with pumpkins ready to be carved into smiling jack-o'-lanterns. Strung between the high windows of the gymnasium was a banner that read:

Go Tigers! Thompson Point High Homecoming, Class of 1995.

She wondered what Rachel was working on and how many unfinished decorations lay strewn about.

A soft breeze whispered across the night, moving

her hair into her face. Sabrina shook her head, ears keen to the sounds around her. She tucked her right hand into her pocket, her fingers on the handle of the Swiss Army knife, ready to draw it out at any second.

Tonight. I can't wait anymore.

The stalker could be anywhere. A lightbulb above the gymnasium door buzzed and illuminated the short step in front of it, bathing it in a warm, yellow hue. Shadows consumed everything beyond the bulb's reach. That was where the stalker operated from. In the inky blackness beyond Sabrina's vision. A creature of forever midnight, hiding in wait.

Another thought struck her as she grabbed the handle on the gymnasium door and pulled it open. *Was there a connection between the stalker and the baby doll? Is that why they always sang lullabies?*

It seemed possible, even if Sabrina couldn't quite pinpoint how some mysterious person or entity could control a doll given to her as a health class project. A curse, maybe? But why? And why her? Was there something she wasn't remembering? Someone she had wronged in some way? Whatever the answer was, it remained in the dark.

Sabrina entered the gymnasium, slamming the door shut behind her. The loud bang echoed out across the dim, empty room.

"Rachel?"

No answer except for the bouncing return of her own voice.

"Hello? Rachel, where are you?"

She took a few shuffling steps forward, not wanting to get too far away from the door in case she needed an exit. Rolling carts of painting supplies, blank posterboards, blue and yellow balloons, tangled strands of ribbons, and clusters of pumpkins littered the basketball court. A streak of blue paint, like it had been spilled, marked a trail toward one of the basketball hoops. Sabrina's eyes followed it across the court. A strange shadow bobbed back and forth where the paint ended. She looked up and screamed, instantly letting go of the backpack handle and falling to her knees.

It was Rachel.

Her body was dangling off the rim of the basketball hoop from a noose tied around her neck. Her throat had been slashed, the rope digging into the wound to open it further. A river of wet blood ran down her front, dripping off her shoes and mixing with the blue paint below.

Most haunting was Rachel's face. Her eyes bulged out of their sockets like wide saucers filled with absolute terror. Specks of blood blotted her beautiful blonde hair like a dye job gone wrong. And her mouth, frozen open in a silent scream.

Sabrina hardly had time to process it, let alone mourn, as a sickening, familiar smell of leather entered her nostrils and the sharp tip of a blade poked into the back of her neck.

"Stand up," a voice breathed in a whispered hiss.

Sabrina did as she was told. The knife stayed with her, as if a part of her skin. Once on her feet, the leather-gloved hand shot out from the shadows behind her and covered her mouth.

"Don't scream. Just move where my knife guides you."

Sabrina kept as calm and quiet as she could and awaited the guidance of the blade. The hand disappeared from her face, and from what she could hear, it sounded like the stalker had picked up her backpack.

They want the baby doll?

"To the basement. Go!" The knife poked further, urging Sabrina forward. She didn't reach for her own weapon just yet. Not with the blade pressed to her skin or the stalker's breath hot on her neck. One wrong move and she'd end up like…

No. She couldn't think about it. She had to stay focused if she was going to get out of this. If she was going to avenge Rachel's death.

"I have waited for this night for so long," the voice said, with a twinge of feverish excitement.

The baby doll piped up from the backpack, joining in with a muffled smattering of babble and nonsense. As the knife pushed her along, Sabrina felt the wet smack of a pair of lips right beside her ear. And then, in a whisper, like some twisted game of telephone, she heard:

"It's almost time for the ritual to begin."

Chapter 24

The knife spurred Sabrina farther into the school, a place that *should* be so familiar to her, practically a second home built into her DNA over the last few years, except now it wasn't. She moved blindly through the darkened maze of hallways. The blade was her set of eyes, its sharp tip steering her toward the unknowable abyss of the basement.

"Easy now, one step at a time," the voice instructed as they reached the staircase that led down into the janitor's lair. To the place where the stalker had first made physical contact. When the same guiding knife had first kissed her throat and claimed her necklace.

Sabrina kept her arms idle at her sides and carefully made the descent, planting both feet firmly on each step before continuing to the next. The knife never wavered, keeping patiently with her as they traversed downward.

"Forward," the voice said at the bottom of the staircase.

The dim lights that had been just enough to lead Sabrina toward the bathroom last time were out. She'd been able to make out faint outlines in the shadowed hallways upstairs, the specters of lockers and doorways. Down here, there was nothing; absolute pitch black. She noticed an immediate drop in temperature, too. The cool breath of the brick walls surrounded her like a swirl of spirits, sending a frosty ripple throughout her bones.

Prodding a bit farther into her skin without drawing blood, the knife forced Sabrina to the right. They were nearing the basement bathroom. The heavy scent of bleach and cleaning chemicals stung her nostrils and throat, causing her eyes to water. She didn't wipe them away, not that it mattered much anyway. She couldn't see anything except . . .

A light up ahead. A thin beam of white light shining through a partially opened door. Sabrina reasoned it must be the maintenance room just beyond the janitor's office. It had to be where they were headed, where the knife had been pushing her to all along. There was nothing else down there.

What was waiting for her in that room? What horrors were housed in those mysterious gloved hands? Was Sabrina supposed to be some sort of sacrifice? Was that what the ritual the stalker had mentioned was all about?

Her stomach twisted into a tangled weave of knots as the glowing slit came closer. A growing fear nearly halted her steps, but the chrome death pressed just above the top of her spine kept her moving. *Something* was waiting for them in the maintenance room. Sabrina could feel a presence, a wrongness in the air. She couldn't quite place it, but she did know that she didn't want to go in there. Suddenly, the Swiss Army knife felt useless, like a toy in her pocket.

"Open the door."

Sabrina hesitated for as many seconds as the knife would allow, which wasn't many.

"NOW!" the stalker spat, impatiently pressing the knife deeper. A stab of pain shot through Sabrina's neck. Wincing, she grabbed a hold of the door and opened it. The sudden bath of light blinded her just as much as the darkness. She raised an arm to shield her eyes and stepped inside.

As she adjusted to the brightness, a workbench set against a wall of hanging tools materialized in her vision. Sabrina saw that the source of light came from a small lamp clamped above the janitor's work station, illuminating it like a theater stage. Everything beyond was shrouded in shadows, and it was there, in the suffocating darkness, that she knew *something* was waiting.

"Lay down on the table."

Sabrina obeyed, and as she lifted herself onto the workbench, the knife retreated from the back of her neck. She lay down on her back, and almost instantly, the stalker's hands went to work tying her ankles to each corner. Then the black leathered fingers grabbed her arms and pulled them back, securing each wrist. Aside from the ability to swivel her head from left to right, she was completely immobile, restrained in a spread-eagle position to the janitor's workbench.

"I've waited *so* long for this moment," the stalker said, stepping away to unzip the backpack and pull out the baby doll. "Years, in fact."

Then, clutching the fake infant that had caused Sabrina so much grief, the stalker crept into the light, hovering above her body. Her eyes darted up at the face smiling down at her. She gasped, zapped with shock at the revelation.

Staring back, with her black shoulder-length hair in disarray and smears of bright red lipstick outlining her mouth like a kid coloring outside the lines, was her health teacher.

"Ms. Pike!?"

"Yes," she answered in a gentle tone, stroking Sabrina's cheek with the side of her hand. "My perfect vessel. I've waited so long for this moment."

Sabrina shuddered at her touch. "Your . . . *what?*"

"Vessel," Ms. Pike said matter-of-factly. "Womb. Surrogate. *You* are going to deliver my precious Andrew. You are going to bring him back to me."

Sabrina was too stunned to speak.

"It wasn't supposed to be like this," Ms. Pike continued. "Life can be so unbelievably cruel."

"I'm sorry for whatever happened to you, but it's *not my fault!* I don't know what you're thinking, but *I* can't bring your baby back."

"*Oh*, that's where you're wrong," Ms. Pike whispered, her messy lips pressed to the poor girl's ear. She gently licked the outer edge of her lobe like a tender lover and then inhaled deeply through her nostrils, as though Sabrina were a bouquet, before pulling away.

Sabrina squirmed, or tried to, but the ropes kept her body pressed tightly onto the workbench. She wanted to puke. She hated that so much more than the graze on her cheek. A way out seemed impossible. How was she supposed to escape the clutches of a *clearly* deranged woman when she was tied up and unable to move? The knife in her pocket was seriously useless now.

When your mind is clear, you'll know where to steer. The words from her mom floated up through the traffic in her brain. Her mind was far from clear, and, given that she was strapped down, there was nowhere to steer. If only she could reach the Swiss Army knife, she would whip it out and plunge the blade straight into her teacher's neck. Instead, she held onto the tiniest glimmer of hope that something would present itself. Until then, the best thing she could do was buy herself time.

"What . . . What happened to you and your baby?" Sabrina asked, doing her best to sound as sincere and empathetic as possible.

Ms. Pike placed a hand over her heart, appearing touched by her student's concern. "I thought you'd never ask," she said, placing the baby doll onto the floor. Sabrina couldn't see it, but a circle had been drawn in chalk beside the workbench. The baby lay still in the center, completely silent. In fact, the only sounds heard now were Ms. Pike as she shuffled about to prepare the ritual.

"We were *supposed* to be a happy little family," Ms. Pike began. Sabrina listened intently, hoping somewhere in her story there would be a vital piece of information that could provide some sort of advantage. "Everything was so perfect. We were going to have our little boy. We decided to name him Andrew, after my husband's father. We were so happy. So in love with our little boy. And then during the delivery, something happened. At first, I had no idea what was going on. The doctor started shouting at the nurses.

Everyone was rushing around me. Yelling. Screaming. 'Hurry! Hurry!' they told me. 'Keep pushing! We have to get this baby out now.' But . . ." Ms. Pike paused, sniffling back tears. She bowed her head. "I wasn't quick enough."

Sabrina said nothing, awaiting the next part of the story. Instead of words, she heard the distinct click of a clasp opening and then a clink of glass bottles touching. From her limited vantage point, she couldn't see what Ms. Pike was doing but could surmise it was something that wouldn't bode well for her.

After an agonizing stretch of waiting and wondering and hearing all the little noises from whatever her teacher was piecing together, Ms. Pike approached the side of the bench. Sabrina shifted her head, and their eyes met. Ms. Pike gazed at her with quivering spheres of sadness, wet and shiny. Running her fingers through Sabrina's hair like an admiring mother standing above a crib, she cleared her throat and continued.

"The umbilical cord had become wrapped around my sweet baby's neck. It was cutting off his airflow. He was suffocating inside me. By the time I pushed him out, he was blue in the face . . . dead."

"I'm so sorry," Sabrina offered, this time genuinely. The sadness in Ms. Pike's voice was like thin ice on a frozen lake, one solid step away from shattering completely.

"It never ends. That emptiness. That desperate longing. I couldn't cope with it. My husband tried to console me, to be there for me. But eventually, he left. Couldn't take it anymore. I don't really blame him. I was beyond repair. *Nothing*, aside from Andrew being warm and healthy in my arms, was going to heal me. With my husband gone, I had no one. I had nothing. I built a shrine for Andrew in my closet, piled with all the clothes he would never get to wear, all the unplayed toys, the empty bottles, my hospital wristband, and his death certificate. I cried and prayed every day, not necessarily to God but to anyone and anything that would listen.

"I wanted my baby back at any cost. Finally, the day came when I'd had enough. I was going to join my baby in the afterlife. As I hung the rope from the ceiling and tested the noose, ready to end it all, something stopped me. An answer from beyond. A . . . a strange portal, a *void*, appeared within the shadows of the closet. And from that void . . . a demon. The one who had heard my prayers and pleas for the return of my baby boy.

"The demon had no name, or at least it didn't introduce itself with one. I don't even know what its true form looks like. What greeted me was a disembodied set of teeth floating in the swirling blackness. *The smile in the darkness* . . . that's what I came to call it. It was there to offer me *exactly* what I wanted. I could have my baby back . . . for a price."

"What was the price?" Sabrina was afraid to ask.

"*Oh*, you'll find out, my perfect vessel, don't you worry."

Ms. Pike's lips widened into a mismatched grin. Sabrina felt a pulse from the shadows beyond her. Whatever it was that had been hiding was coming forward. The curtain of everlasting night was closing in on her.

And then she saw it. Taking shape in the space above Ms. Pike's head. A set of teeth levitating in the air.

The smile in the darkness.

"It's time for me to make good on my end of the bargain!"

In the black expanse, the teeth curved upward into a menacing grin.

Heart pumped full of fear, Sabrina made a futile attempt to wrench free from the ropes binding her, screaming at the top of her lungs for help.

Chapter 25

"Why me?" Sabrina sputtered. "What did I do?"

"The ritual requires a host," Ms. Pike answered. "I knew it would be you almost immediately. Ever since we first met during your freshman year, I never forgot about you. You're so . . . *perfect*. Even back then, as a new student at Thompson Point High, I could see your potential. I *knew* you would become valedictorian and head cheerleader. There were never any doubts in my mind about you."

"But I'm not perfect!"

"Don't be so coy! You *know* you are. You relish it. I can see it on your face and the way you carry yourself. Being on top is what suits you best. You're the perfect vessel to bring my baby back to me."

The teeth gnashed together in the air like the snap of an angered dog.

Ms. Pike held up the stolen choker necklace. The lioness charm glinted in the dim light from the workbench lamp. Sabrina felt a power emanating from it. A ferocious energy teeming in its silver eyes and shining fangs.

"First, a personal object. I'm sure this necklace looks familiar?"

Ms. Pike placed it in the circle, draping it across the baby doll's neckline.

"Next, a sample of skin or hair."

A tuft of Sabrina's hair appeared in her hands, plucked from a side pocket on her satchel. She knelt and positioned it atop the doll's bald head.

The sound of clinking glass returned. Ms. Pike held up three vials, each containing a red liquid. Sabrina didn't need to ask what it was. She already knew.

"Probably the most important requirement of all. The blood of three. The demon demands sacrifice."

Ms. Pike popped the top off one of the vials.

"Christopher," she said, pouring the blood out onto the baby doll.

Hearing his name and realizing that was *his* blood brought tears to the forefront of Sabrina's eyes. She thought of him then, imagining him all sweaty in his Thompson Point Tigers uniform after having scored the winning touchdown at the homecoming game. She shut her eyes and focused, trying to send another ripple of love his way. Maybe, just maybe, despite his coma, he would sense her desperation and feel her wave and send one back. If demons could be summoned to bring back a dead baby, why couldn't a coma patient receive and send brainwave communications? At this point, *everything* seemed possible to Sabrina.

The next vial was opened.

"Lawrence," Ms. Pike announced.

The blood in Rachel's driveway—that was from Lawrence!

Ms. Pike tipped the vial, and its contents spilled

out onto the baby doll's chest, pooling with Christopher's blood.

Now it was time for the final vial. The teeth chattered in anticipation.

"I'm sure you can guess whose blood this is," Ms. Pike teased.

Of course, Sabrina knew. It was her best friend. The one she'd seen not even an hour prior, hanging from the rim of the basketball hoop. Her stomach dropped as the images of Rachel's dead, terrified face returned to haunt her. Ms. Pike tilted her wrist and emptied the blood into the circle.

The floating mouth seemed to enjoy this, spreading its black-hole lips to reveal even more teeth.

"Almost complete," Ms. Pike announced with a giddy zip to her voice. She crouched down to rub the baby doll's blood-soaked belly. "Don't worry, Andrew, you'll be with mommy again very soon."

Fixated on Christopher, Rachel, and Lawrence, Sabrina was hurled back to the grim reality of the school basement when she felt a warmth on her stomach and realized her shirt was being lifted. Ms. Pike, hovering above, her face distorted by shadows, had partially pulled the garment to expose her midriff. Having ditched the leather gloves some time ago, she delicately ran her pointer finger along Sabrina's belly, skin to skin.

"Andrew's soul has been so restless and lonely inside that baby doll. He's ready to be born again."

Sabrina could only watch in wide-eyed terror as Ms. Pike produced her knife once more, raising it toward the light as if to ensure it was real. The blade shimmered in response. "The final step," she said, holding her left arm an inch above Sabrina's midriff, "flesh of the asker."

With the ferocity and quickness of a hungry predator, Ms. Pike brought the blade down into her arm, cutting into the skin between her elbow and wrist. Sabrina screamed as if she were the one getting stabbed as blood seeped from the wound and spilled onto her stomach. The warm red liquid traveled down her sides, leaking into her pants and underwear and pooling in her belly button.

Ms. Pike worked the knife, grunting as if she were a mechanic trying to wrench a corroded bolt loose, until she had successfully removed a piece of flesh from her arm. She wiped it across Sabrina's skin, smearing the blood like ultrasound jelly. Then she stepped back, her lips bent in a crooked smile, basking in her completion of the ritual as she awaited the rebirth of her son.

The lamp above began to flicker. A swell of breath, like a rumbling storm, poured out of the demon. Tools trembled and fell off the wall as the entire building began to shake. Ms. Pike rejoiced, raising her arms in praise. The floating teeth, *the smile in the darkness*, continued to exercise its power, grinning and growling.

And then Sabrina felt it. A kick in her stomach. She lifted her head as much as she could, tucking her chin against her collarbone and nearly fainted at what she saw.

Her belly was *growing*. It expanded rapidly, like a balloon being filled, until it was so swollen that Sabrina could no longer see her legs. Something wriggled inside of her, pushing on her intestines and pressing against her pregnant skin. The thing inside wanted out. It thrashed and pounded, like a rabid animal locked in a cage. She could see the tips of tiny fingers protruding and the outline of a face trying to break through.

"No," she pleaded, "please no!"

Andrew.

The demon had transferred him into her. It had resurrected Ms. Pike's dead baby.

"Yes!" her teacher cheered, with tears of joy leaking down her face. "Come on, Andrew! Just rip right through! You can do it! Mommy wants to hold you *so* bad! That's it, you can . . ."

CRACK!

Through labored breaths, Sabrina heard a loud grunt, followed by the *swoosh* of something heavy, like a baseball bat, swinging in the air. A second after, the sickening, wet sound of contact, of pulverized flesh and misting blood. And then, the audible *thud* of a body, or something equally as heavy, dropping to the floor.

"Sabrina!" a voice called out. It was familiar, but her brain was clouded and could not make the connection. She glanced over as the baby's fingernails dug into the inner lining of her belly. The fuzzy silhouette standing before her slowly came into view.

"Gina?"

"Yeah," she answered, holding the metallic bat at the ready. "Like what the hell is going on here!?"

"No time to explain, just help me, please!" Sabrina said, wincing in pain. "Grab the Swiss Army knife from my pocket and get this thing out of me!"

"Like . . . you want me to cut you?" Gina gasped, trembling with hesitation.

"Yes!"

Gina stepped closer and cautiously eyed Sabrina's throbbing belly. She saw the impression of a forehead, nose, and cheek as it pressed full force against her exposed skin.

"What is that!?"

"Gina, hurry! Grab the knife and kill this thing before *it* kills *me*!"

Still nervous but realizing there wasn't any more time to waste, Gina shoved her fingers into Sabrina's pocket and retrieved the tool. She opened the blade and held it high, trying her best to keep it steady.

"Are you ready?"

"YES!" Sabrina yelled, straining against the gnashing and clawing of the baby and preparing herself for the inevitable pain of the knife.

"Okay," Gina said, exhaling deeply. "One, two, three, GO!"

She thrust the blade downward, stabbing through the skin and into the baby's forehead. Gina felt it hit bone and withdrew the knife. Blood leaked out from the newly made slit in Sabrina's bulbous belly. She struck again and again, plunging the knife as deep as it would go, widening the wound with each stab.

"Take it out!" Sabrina cried, wincing in pain. "Get this thing out of me!"

Gina nodded and readied herself once more. She placed the knife onto the workbench beside Sabrina, rolled up her right sleeve and plunged her hand into the slit in Sabrina's belly. Warm blood coursed and oozed between her fingers as she blindly groped around for the baby's skull. Gina felt the thundering vibrations from Sabrina's rapid heartbeat, pulsing like an underground tremor. And then, her fingers grazed something both soft and thick—the baby's head. She closed her fingers around it like a claw machine and wrenched her arm from the wound. She lost her grip, slipping off from the slickness of the blood. The baby's head peered out from the incision like a prairie dog and let out a scream.

In the dim light, Gina could see the knife marks in its head and the blood that ran down its face. Regaining focus, she reached down and pushed her fingers back inside Sabrina, against the baby's backside to force it out. She pulled and forced it free, holding the bloody newborn beneath its armpits.

"Kill it!" Sabrina yelled. "You have to kill that thing!"

Gina moved with a force beyond her own, as if she were nothing but a puppet with someone else pulling the strings. She plucked the knife from the spot she'd left it and without any hesitation at all, forced the blade into the baby's chest. She repeated the motion again and again, only stopping when the pained wail that screeched from its lips registered in her ears.

In response, she dropped the knife and it clattered to the floor, lost to the shadows.

The cry echoed out into the room. Gina paused, still holding the baby up, as a blue mist seeped out from its stab wounds, rising like smoky fingers before dissipating into the darkness. And with it, the teeth disappeared too, slinking back into the shadows from whence they came.

Was that Andrew's spirit? Sabrina wondered as she watched the mist float up and away.

Gina placed the now limp body onto the floor and then jumped back into action and sliced away the rope tied around Sabrina's wrists and ankles. She helped her sit up, slowly and carefully.

"I know you're in bad shape, but we, like, gotta get you outta here," Gina said.

Clutching her bleeding belly, Sabrina nodded and scooted off the workbench. Gina held her by the shoulders, making sure she didn't faint or fall. They stepped over Ms. Pike, who lay in a heap on the cold floor as blood dribbled from the injury on the side of her head. Gina wasn't sure if she was dead or not, but she didn't want to stick around and find out either. Once they got out of there, she would call the cops, and they could either haul her off to jail or the morgue.

Time had lost all meaning to Sabrina, but eventually they made it out, stumbling through the entrance doors and out onto the grass in front of the school. Her belly had shrunk back to its normal size, but the stab wounds remained. She pressed hard onto them with her shirt, applying as much pressure as her weakened muscles could muster.

"I'll be right back, I'm going to call for help" Gina said, running off toward the payphone across the lot.

As Sabrina sat and waited, a breeze interrupted the otherwise calm and quiet night, mussing her hair. As it passed, she could have sworn she heard her name whispered within.

"Sabrina."

It sounded like Christopher, though whether it

was an actual response from her boyfriend or merely a hopeful delusion, she wasn't sure. The gust passed, and the air settled back into its serene state, with the crickets chirping and the stars twinkling above. It was Christopher, she decided, sending her a signal.

Love is the most healing energy of all.

Gina's footsteps pounded across the pavement as she hurried back, huffing and puffing.

"The police ... and ambulance ... are, like, on their way ..." she said, trying to catch her breath. Once she had recuperated, Gina plopped down beside Sabrina and placed an arm around her shoulder. "So ... care to, like, fill me in on what just happened?"

Sabrina didn't answer. Instead, she leaned her head to rest on Gina's shoulder and closed her eyes. Together, the girls waited in silence for the sound of sirens to come rushing up the hill.

Chapter 26

Days later, Sabrina opened her eyes from a nap in her hospital bed. Her stomach wounds were stitched up, but still sore and would be for some time. The doctors had said she was lucky that all her vital organs were missed. It hurt to move, and she tried her best not to.

Her mom and dad were right by her side and had been since they'd received the call from the police that their daughter had been attacked.

"Are you thirsty, sweetheart?" her mom asked, picking up a styrofoam cup of water resting on the windowsill.

"That would be great, thank you," Sabrina replied. Every time she fell asleep in the hospital, she woke with a dry mouth. Her mom helped insert the straw between her parched lips, then held the cup as Sabrina gulped the glorious liquid down.

Once satiated, her mom took the cup away and sat back down, scooting her chair closer to hold her daughter's hand. Her dad joined in, scraping his chair across the linoleum flooring to the opposite side of her bed.

"How are you feeling?" He gently brushed her hair with the side of his hand.

"Like I got stabbed multiple times," Sabrina answered with a smirk.

"*Ah*, but they can't kill your wit," her dad said, and they shared a laugh together. Her wounds made the laughter hurt, but it was a pain that she welcomed.

Sabrina grabbed the remote from the side of her bed and turned on the little TV suspended from the ceiling. The screen flickered to life with a fuzzy image of a game show audience clapping and smiling as the announcer said, "Lorraine Dawson, come on down, you're the next contestant on *The Price Is Right!*" Her parents loved this show. She set the remote beside her on the bed, and they watched together as Bob Barker asked the contestants to place their bids on a brand-new refrigerator.

"Fourteen hundred!" her mom blurted out. "I saw that exact same fridge last week at *Sears*."

"Fourteen-oh-one!" her dad rebutted.

Sabrina somewhat rolled her eyes, but really, it was charming. Her parents always played along, and her dad *always* bid one dollar higher than her mom. More often than not, it worked out for him.

As the game show played on the TV, Sabrina zoned out, distracted by an onrush of thoughts from the last few days. From what she had gathered, after talking with the police numerous times and giving statements, Ms. Pike had survived the blow to the head. The officers had found her in the maintenance room, covered in blood and calling out for Andrew. They arrested her, but instead of jail, she was being sent away to a mental facility. Though for how long, she had no idea. There was never any mention of a dead baby being discovered alongside her. Sabrina wondered what had happened to it. Did the body disappear like the blue mist that had curled out of its wounds? She didn't waste too much time contemplating that fact. It didn't matter. It was over with . . . at least she *hoped* it was.

Thompson Point was reeling with shock and sadness. People could not believe a teacher could lose her mind like that and murder students. A candlelight vigil was held for Lawrence and Rachel. Christopher was still in a coma, but they included him as well, praying for him to wake up. Sabrina wished she could have been there, but she was confined in the hospital for a few more days at least. Once she was out and able, she would hold her own memorial for Rachel. Lawrence, too. They didn't deserve what happened to them.

Someone knocked on the door.

"Come on in," Sabrina said.

The door swung open, and Gina popped her head in with an enthusiastic wave.

"Hello, how are we doing?" she asked. "I have a surprise for you. Well, like, two surprises really."

Gina momentarily stepped out into the hallway and returned a second later, pushing a wheelchair.

"Christopher!" Sabrina cried, instantly brought to tears.

"I'm so glad to see you," Christopher said. Sabrina's dad moved aside so Gina could wheel him up close.

Christopher reached forward and grabbed Sabrina's hand. She missed his touch immensely, and seeing him awake caused her heart to swell.

"Did you feel my love ripples?" she whispered, slightly embarrassed for Gina and her parents to hear.

"Your what?" Christopher gave her a puzzled stare.

"Never mind. I'm just so glad you're alive."

"I'm glad you are, too."

"You can thank Gina for that. She saved my life."

"Who would have thought?"

"By the way," Sabrina said, lifting her head slightly to look past Christopher at Gina, "how did you know I was down there?"

"I didn't initially. I saw you pull into the parking lot that night. I ended up turning around because I thought you might, like, be trying to sabotage my Homecoming decoration plans. Then I found . . . well, *you know*. And I heard all this, like, commotion coming from somewhere, so I grabbed a baseball bat just in case and followed the sounds. That's when I found out Ms. Pike had you tied up."

"I really can't thank you enough."

"Don't mention it," Gina said, blushing.

"So what's my other surprise?"

"*Oh!* Right . . . Hold on."

Gina dashed out of the room once more and returned with a bulging bouquet of white flowers. She strode over and handed them to Sabrina.

"*Oh my gosh*, you shouldn't have! Not after all you've already done."

"Those aren't from me. A nurse asked me if I wouldn't mind bringing those up to you when I arrived. Said they were, like, delivered to the front desk and addressed to you."

"*Oh*," Sabrina said, a little unsure. "Well, whoever sent them, they are really nice."

"Baby's breath," her mom said.

"*Huh?*"

"The flowers. They are supposed to symbolize purity and new beginnings."

"I think I see a card tucked into the side there," her dad said. "Why don't you see who it's from?"

Everyone leaned forward as Sabrina plucked the card from the bouquet, eager to learn the identity of the sender. On the outside of the plain white card was her name written in elegant cursive. As she opened it and read the message inside, a crippling fear overtook her. The card fell from her fingers and landed in her lap. On the monitor, her heartbeat began to rapidly increase. Sabrina let out an ear-shattering scream. The words would haunt her forever.

Rest well, my perfect vessel.

ACKNOWLEDGMENTS

There's so many I would like to thank for helping make this book possible. Firstly, to my family, Kelly and Levi, for your unwavering support and belief. To E.D. Black for being an absolute homie and beta reader. To Judith Sonnet, for the advice and enthusiasm. To Caleb J. Pecue and Austin Hinderliter at Terrorcore Publishing for supporting me and believing in this idea. And to everyone on my ARC team, thank you so much for your time and passion. I really, truly appreciate it more than words can say.

ABOUT THE AUTHOR

A.D. Aro lives in Salisbury, Massachusetts. He has been a fan of all things spooky his whole life, raised on *Goosebumps*, *Are You Afraid of the Dark* and the VHS box art from the horror section of the video rental stores. Currently, he writes a middle grade horror series called *Bumps In The Night*. *Baby's Breath* is his first YA horror novel. He welcomes questions and comments at:

bumpsinthenightbooks@gmail.com

www.ingramcontent.com/pod-product-compliance
Lightning Source LLC
LaVergne TN
LVHW032005070526
838202LV00058B/6298